#CoolGrannies

Who's Driving?

Susan Allison-Dean

ISBN 13: 978-1546815334
ISBN 10: 1546815333

Cover design and interior formatting by Deborah Bradseth, Tugboat Design

This novel is dedicated to all the cool women who inspire us to grow old with grace, laughter and a touch of sassiness.

Acknowledgements

Special thanks to the members of my weekly writing group: Anne, Liz, Pat, Jinny and Marion, your critiques, friendship and laughter made this book possible.

Big hug to my husband, Robert, and furry son, Bubba, their love and companionship help in between the lines of writing.

I am deeply grateful to the amazing, patient, and incredibly talented, Deborah Bradseth from Tugboat Design.

To the real Maretta, a woman ahead of her time, whose loss made me wonder and inspired this story.

Chapter 1

"I think she's gone crazy! You need to come over here right away," Joan whispered into the kitchen phone as she peaked over her shoulder to see if her best and oldest friend, Maretta, could hear her.

"Why, what is she doing?" Connie asked.

"Who are you talking to?" Maretta yelled from her bedroom.

"I think she's coming, just come over here now," Joan whispered urgently then hung up the phone. She took a deep breath, smoothed her silver-grey hair back and tried to look innocent. "No one, just talking to myself."

Maretta scanned her bedroom one last time. Her eyes paused on the queen-sized bed made of walnut. The chocolate-brown-stained frame matched the bedside tables as well as the his-and-hers bureaus. She could hear her mother's words even though they were almost fifty-years old, "Your father and I have decided to give you and Charles a bedroom set as a wedding gift. There's no sense in buying you a set of china. It's not like you are going to be entertaining executives."

Charlie chuckled when Maretta shared the news with him. "We'll have a lot more fun with a bed than china."

Maretta smiled so Charlie's feelings wouldn't be hurt. In truth, she couldn't care less what her parents gave her. *If only they loved him as much as I did,* she remembered thinking. The old wound on her heart was now covered with a well-healed scar.

She turned and looked into her sad eyes in the mirror above her bureau. She leaned in close and let her finger trace one of the crevices that led from the side of her eye to her temple.

"Be glad you have those, it took a lot of laughs to get them," Charlie always told her.

She reached down, opened the jar of anti-aging cream and applied it gently to her face in smooth strokes. The floral scent transcended her thoughts to her rose garden outside. As she massaged the residual lotion into her hands, she felt something inside beckon her to open her jewelry box.

She opened the hand carved treasure chest, a gift from Charlie, and gingerly sifted through the pieces like she was looking for a seashell in a pile of sand. She stopped when she found the silver locket that lay near the bottom. Gently, she removed it and held it in her hand. Her thumb caressed the tarnished flower engraved on the front of the heart as if she was reading braille. With her pink-painted fingernail, she flicked the locket open. Charlie's young, smiling, chiseled face greeted her.

Maretta reminisced alone as her heart ached.

"I have something for you." Charlie handed her a black velvet bag as they sat parked by Cranberry Lake. Inside was a black leather box.

It's much too early for a ring, *she thought as her palms began to sweat.* We've only been dating for six months. *Cautiously, she opened the box. Relief flooded her veins when she saw the heart-shaped locket. She pulled it up by the chain and let the heart dangle before her.*

"It's beautiful," she said. Then she opened it. "But, there is nothing in it."

"You can put a picture that you like inside," Charlie said as he sat turned towards her with one arm resting on the hard ship-sized steering wheel.

Maretta turned towards him and said softly, "I need a picture of you."

They locked eyes. Charlie reached his hand up and caressed her check. "I was hoping you would want that."

He leaned closer towards her. Maretta met him half way. Their lips touched tenderly at first, then more eagerly.

Maretta shivered at the memory of how she felt like a child lighting the Christmas tree for the holiday. That's when she knew. This is my man.

Maretta closed the locket and slipped the necklace around her neck. She tapped the heart, stood upright, and whispered, "Come on, we're going for a ride."

Joan returned to the master bedroom where she found Maretta rummaging through drawers, selecting various wear and stuffing it into a vanilla-colored laundry bag with a tie string on it. Maretta didn't even look up at her, focused instead on her mission. In the more than forty years they had known each other, Joan had never seen Maretta like this. It worried her deeply.

"Don't you have a suitcase?"

"Suitcase," Maretta snarked. "For what? We never went anywhere."

Joan peaked down the hallway hoping to see a cavalry coming but knowing full well that Connie could not have gotten here that fast. The hallway was dimly lit. A well-worn runner, with tassels half chewed off the ends, lined the floor. A blended scent of musty old and cat arose from it. The dark paneling that Maretta complained about every spring still holding the walls up.

Joan could hear Maretta in her head mocking Charlie, "Why change it, it looks good. If you paint it, we'll have to paint it every few years to keep it looking nice. Just polish it." *Well, at least now, Maretta can paint it any color she wants*, Joan thought.

"Guess what," Joan shouted.

Maretta didn't answer. She was in the closet, sliding hangers of clothes with urgency.

"You can paint that hallway now. I'll help you. What color would you like to change it to?"

Maretta came out with two dresses slung over her arm and a pair of worn-leather heels. "I don't give a shit about that hallway. I'm not spending another day in this house."

"But where are you planning to go?"

"Anywhere. Anywhere but here. Seventy-two years in the same town is more than enough." Maretta slid the hangers from the dresses, tossed them on the unmade bed, rolled the dresses into logs and stuffed them into the laundry bag.

The sound of the back door slamming brought relief, at least to Joan. Connie hurried into the room, somewhat out of breath. Joan cringed a bit when she saw Ann following behind her, knowing Ann was not going to be any help in this situation.

When Connie saw the bag with clothes bulging out of it, she stopped and looked cautiously over at Joan. Their eyes met and secretly conversed.

"What is going on?" Ann asked. Slowly, she unwound the hand knit silk scarf that was neatly arranged around her neck.

An awkward silence filled the room. Maretta began picking through the make up on her bureau.

"Where are you going, Maretta?" Ann asked after sizing up the situation. She moved a few steps closer.

"Away from here," Maretta replied fervently, without looking at any of them. She opened the top drawer of the bureau, retrieved a long sock and stuffed a tube of foundation, a compact and two sticks of lipstick in it. "Going to see the world."

"But you just buried your husband. For God's sake, his body probably isn't even cold yet." Ann pleaded. Her bleach-blond hair was perfectly styled, as always, in a shoulder length bob.

"What the hell do you know? You've traveled the world. London this, Rome that, 'Oh, how lovely Washington is when the cherry blossoms are in bloom,'" Maretta imitated Ann's uppity voice and held her nose up as she turned to stare at her. She didn't need reminding that her husband was dead. The graphic image of Charlie lying, contorted on the bathroom floor with his boxers around his ankles, replayed over and over in her head. Massive heart attack they told her.

Ann stood frozen.

Connie softened, walked gently up to Maretta, and put her hand on her shoulder. With a tilted head she said, "Honey, traveling is a good idea. Maybe you just want to give it some time though. Take some time to grieve."

Maretta broke away, stomped over to the laundry bag and forced the sock full of make up inside. "I'm not dead yet and if I wait any longer, I might be. I'm leaving tomorrow morning and no one is stopping me."

Before Connie could add any more rebuttals, Joan jumped in, "I'm going with you."

Maretta turned to look at Joan to see if she was really serious.

Connie turned and looked at Joan with her mouth gaping wide open.

Ann put her hand firmly on her hip as she snapped, "What in the world would you do that for?"

"Maretta's right. We're not getting any younger." Joan raised her head high, authoritatively. "I could use some adventure. I keep sitting around hoping my son and daughter-in-law will invite me to help with the new baby and my grandson, but her mother is hoarding them. I can't get kid time no matter how much I plead with my son. Why should I sit around here?"

"To properly travel one needs to plan," Ann waved her hand in the air. "If you're going to drive, you need to map out where you're going, what you want to see, where you will stay. You don't want to get stuck somewhere shady you know."

"I'm not doing that," Maretta pulled the strings tight to close the laundry bag. "Ruins the fun of it."

Ann took a deep breath and clenched her lips.

"But what about your cat?" Connie asked as she walked over and stroked the feline.

"Rustle? He's going to stay with the neighbors, I've already arranged that." The orange tabby lounged on the pillow at the head of the bed, indifferent to the conversation.

"It's settled then, anyone else coming along?" Joan cut in. Her steel-grey, blue eyes looked at each of them like a drill sergeant.

The ladies looked from one to another.

Connie shifted her stance. "It does kind of sound like fun, but things are going pretty well with Harold, I think I'm going to stick around here." She scrunched her shoulders to her head like a giddy schoolgirl.

"Going well? Do tell," Joan tilted her head and raised her eyebrows.

Up until now, they hadn't pressured Connie about her new relationship. They knew it had taken her a good ten years to even consider dating again, even though she did have several suitors. When Connie lost the love of her life she was devastated even though Joe's death was no surprise. In fact, it was a shock to all Connie's friends that he held on so long. Ten years with Parkinson's. It was torture to see the once jovial guy slowly morph into a bedbound, adult-sized infant.

Connie blushed. "Well, if you must know, Harold got a prescription for Viagra."

"Viagra!" Joan howled, as the others chimed in with laughter. Joan added, "Woo, hoo! Connie is going to get lucky!"

"Connie, dear, don't get your hopes up," Ann said in her matter-of-fact tone, "Don't you know it shrinks and dries up down there? It will be worse than your first time."

"Ann, why are you always being such a hope dasher, dream smasher?" Maretta snarled. "What do you know?"

"Actually, Ann is right. I talked to my doctor and he prescribed some estrogen cream."

Maretta shot Ann an *I told you so* look.

Ann ignored her, "I hope you use a condom. You know AIDS is growing more rampant amongst our generation."

"Please," Maretta countered. "If we got AIDS today at our age, we'll be dead of something else before that gets us. Look at Magic Johnson. Go have a good time, Connie, you deserve it." With that Maretta hurled her bag onto the floor.

"Good for you, Connie. I better get going home and pack my stuff. You won't leave without me, will you Maretta?" asked Joan.

"8am, I'm leaving. Be here by then or I will leave without you."

"You're all crazy," Ann muttered as she turned and walked toward the kitchen door.

Connie hugged Maretta. "I hope you find what you're looking for. Be careful."

"Don't you worry, we're going to have the time of our lives," Maretta pulled away and thrust her fists in the air. "We'll call and let you know what were up to once in a while."

"Actually, I just learned how to text, my son taught me. We can even text you pictures." Joan pulled her phone out of her pocket.

"I don't know if mine does that," Connie replied.

"Sure it does. Here, I'll show you." Joan reached her hand out and Connie retrieved her cell phone from her pocketbook. She handed Joan her phone. Joan snapped a picture of herself, found her own number, tapped send message, typed 'Bon Voyage' in the box and then hit send while the other two looked on. Within seconds Joan's phone chimed and she proudly showed them the result. "See. We'll send you pictures."

"I don't know how to take a picture," Connie said as she turned to see if Maretta knew how.

Maretta scrunched her lips and shook her head no. "I don't even have one of those fancy phones. Mine calls. That's it. Charlie always said I just needed one just in case of an emergency."

"Well, we'll deal with that when we return," Joan led the way out the backdoor.

Chapter 2

Joan's orchid collection sat on a three-tiered, metal plant holder in front of the southern facing window in her dining room. The lush green leaves, new flower buds, and roots overflowing over the clay pots. One by one, she poured fresh water from the copper watering can tenderly over the bark chips they were planted in. She missed caring for people. After her knee replacement, she was forced to retire from the nursing home.

"I know you don't like too much water," she told her green friends, "but I'm going to give you a little extra because I'm not sure when I will be back. In fact, I'm not sure of a lot of things at the moment."

She stood back and admired her collection. Each one represented a special memory — Mother's Days, Birthdays, and Valentine's Days. On the top shelf a row of framed pictures sat. Joan put the watering can down and picked up the frame in the center. Three men in their young forties beamed smiles at her, while they wrapped arms around each other's shoulders. Paul her only son, with dark, slicked back hair in the center, flanked by Maretta's sons. Glen, always the worrier, had early onset salt-and-pepper-colored hair. Andy, sixteen months younger than the other two, with his casual boyish charm, stood a few inches shorter than the other two.

It was through the oldest boys that Joan and Maretta met. Joan could remember the introduction like it was yesterday. They were two brand-new moms eagerly looking into the hospital nursery window at their newborn sons. The more they shared with each other, the more they found they had in common. Each had to delay having children having due to the Vietnam War; they both loved the Carol Burnett Show and they had mothers who weren't ready to accept that they were in the grandparent club.

Unexpectedly, anger began to seep into Joan as she stared at the photo taken just last Christmas. The past days events began replaying in her head.

"When are you guys heading back?" Paul asked as he heaped potato salad on his plate.

"Day after tomorrow," Andy replied. He perused the buffet table and settled on an egg salad sandwich.

"Me too," Glen added.

"So soon?" Paul questioned, concern in his voice.

Joan pretended to add cream to her coffee at the table in the corner, careful not to let her son and his two best friends know that she was eavesdropping. The funeral guests chatting in the background made it hard to hear what they were saying. She felt guilty she wasn't helping Connie in the kitchen, but something the shock of hearing that Maretta's sons planned on leaving so quickly left her stunned.

"I have a big gig Saturday in Austin," Andy said. "Wedding season, ya know? I feel really bad that I can't stay longer and be with mom."

"Thursday was the only flight I could get back to LA. I wish I could stay longer, but I've got to get back to work Monday. I left everyone in a lurch leaving so suddenly when I got the call about Dad." Glen took a slow deep breath and slowly exhaled.

The three met at the end of the table and each piled a heap of salad onto their plates.

"Will your mom be okay?" Paul whispered.

Andy peered at his older brother. Glen looked out at the living room where his mother sat on the couch, talking to a neighbor. She looks tired, he thought, and older. For the first time he noticed she wasn't disguising her gray roots anymore.

Joan stood still like a statue except for her head, which was now straining to hear what the boys were saying. She lost her balance and her coffee cup rattled in the saucer.

"You'll keep an eye on her won't you, Aunt Joan?" Glen asked hopefully, just noticing her presence. Although not blood related, they were closer than most relatives.

Busted, Joan steadied herself. The full-grown men's eyes looked as sweet and innocent as when they were in kindergarten, and as scared as they were on their first day of school.

"Of course," she reassured them, not sure what else to say. She wanted to reprimand them for not putting their mother ahead of their careers. But, weren't they in shock, too, from the sudden loss of their father?

"See, she's in good hands," Andy said as he grabbed a napkin and headed for the living room. The other two followed behind.

Joan looked at the table overflowing with food, sandwich platters, every salad type you can imagine, a crock-pot of meatballs, bread, lasagna, an unidentified casserole, and deviled eggs. There was enough to feed the entire town. By nights end, most of them will have probably come by, she thought.

Sipping her coffee, she glanced out to check on Maretta who was now talking to Charlie's sister, Barbara. Barbara sat holding on to a small package of tissues for dear life. Eyeliner smudged under her eyes, her feet like water balloons stuffed into shoes. Cardiac disease must run in the family, Joan surmised.

Tom Kisco stood waving his hands in the corner, surrounded by Charlie's old buddies. Some of them bent over grabbing their bellies. That Tom, Joan shook her head, always telling those plumber jokes. Charlie would have liked that.

"What are we going to do with all this food?" Connie asked, startling Joan.

Joan shrugged, "If it doesn't all get eaten, we'll pack some up for Maretta and the boys, then send the rest home with the last guests."

"Poor Maretta. How is she going to manage without him?" Connie asked.

"The same way we did," Joan lifted her chin and looked Connie in the eye. "One day at a time, one hurdle at a time."

"I guess you're right," Connie answered as she bit her

bottom lip. Her permed, white hair, blue eyes, and warm, apple-pie essence often attracted comments of how she resembled Betty White. "At least she has her boys."

Joan kept the boys conversation to herself. No sense in disrupting the reception, although she was starting to simmer inside.

By nine o'clock the last guests dribbled out the front door. Maretta had given up making rounds hours ago. She sat on the blue and green, plaid living room couch and let the grieving guests come to her to bid their farewells.

"Again, we're deeply sorry for your loss," Roland stood over Maretta, his eyes sincere. Ann held her husband's arm tight as if she might fall otherwise.

"Yes, if there's anything we can do just let us know. We're here for you." Ann added.

Maretta couldn't even fudge a smile. "Thanks," was the best she could muster. Easy for her to say, she still has her husband.

As the door closed behind the last guest, Maretta let her head fall back on the couch and closed her eyes. She drew a slow deep breath as she listened to her friends puttering away in the dining room, clanking dishes and speaking softly.

"Get rid of it all," Maretta muttered.

"What did you say, honey?" Connie asked as she came closer.

"I said, get rid of it all. All that food. Don't save any of it." Maretta said sternly. "But you can save it," Connie tried, "and then you'll have food for you and the boys."

"I said, get rid of it all." She leaned forward and looked at her hands, then added, "Please."

Joan looked on. Her eyebrows raised slightly. It wasn't like Maretta to refuse an already prepared meal. She never loved cooking. She should have known then that Maretta was up to something. A cold chill fluttered in the room despite being early June. They gathered the trays, bowls and dishes and brought them into the kitchen, while Maretta returned to the couch.

"We're going to O'Malleys for a bit," Paul announced. Glen and Andy followed him towards the front door.

Andy stopped and went back to give his mother a hug and a peck on the cheek, "Don't wait up."

The door closed behind them before the ladies could contest. The chill in the air got colder.

"They seem to be handling Charlie's death well," Connie said.

Too well, Joan stewed.

Maretta didn't say anything. She got up slowly and headed to the kitchen and retrieved a black hefty bag. She held it wide open next to the table and instructed, "All of it."

Joan placed the photo back on the shelf. "You know what, we should go on an adventure," she told the plants, emphasizing the word should. "Hell, we shouldn't even tell the boys that we are going. Let's see how long it takes them to notice that we are gone."

Chapter 3

Maretta entered her bedroom and took one last look to see if she was forgetting anything. Blinds drawn, jewelry stowed in the safe deposit box at the bank, bed made. Her eyes rest on the queen-size bed. Her mind reminisced of the times she and Charlie shared in that bed; passionate, newlywed lovemaking, baby-making sex, and sexless, interrupted nights of sleep during their sons' early years. When her memory reached their final night together, she turned away abruptly as her throat clenched.

"Maretta!" Joan called as the backdoor slammed behind her.

"Screw it," Maretta mumbled to herself. "If I forget something, I'll just buy it." She shut the bedroom door behind her, stomped to the coat closet, grabbed a light jacket and joined Joan in the kitchen.

"Ready?" Joan asked.

"Let's get the hell out of here," Maretta said, then herded Joan outside and locked the kitchen door behind them.

Joan stood by the trunk of Maretta's old Honda. Maretta

followed her slowly, lugging her laundry bag behind her, but she stopped halfway and dropped her bag in the middle of the driveway.

Is she having second thoughts? Joan wondered. She remained silent, allowing her friend room for her thoughts. The neighbor's kids jumped in the pool next door. Someone else down the street ran a lawnmower.

Maretta's eyes looked at her car, then she looked over at the two-car garage. Leaving the bag right where it was, Maretta sauntered over to the garage. She bent down and shimmied the right door open, then reached for her back in pain.

The gleaming white vision was unveiled. Sofia. Charlie named his prized possession after the bombshell actress, Sofia Loren. "Her taillights remind me of Sofia's big, brown eyes," Charlie used to say.

Yeah, right, Maretta would think to herself. *I think it reminds him of something lower on her body than her eyes.*

"We're taking this one," Maretta stated, as she straightened herself up tall.

Joan's mouth dropped. "Charlie's car? Sofia? Have you ever driven it?"

"Once," Maretta went to retrieve her bag, opened the door and tucked it on the floor behind the drivers seat. She waved her friend to do the same. "Charlie let me drive it once when we were dating."

Joan didn't dare question her decision. *Just go with it,* she told herself.

"I'll pull it out, it will be easier for you to get in." Maretta reached for the keys on a hook, and then disappeared into the car. The engine refused to start. Joan felt like she was watching a dog try to pull its master on a leash, in the wrong direction. The car complained over and over as Maretta stubbornly tried to start it. Fumes gushed from the exhaust pipe.

A knot started to form in Joan's stomach. *Maybe this was a sign?*

After a brief pause, Maretta turned the key as hard as she could, refusing to allow the engine to reject her.

"Vroom! Vroom!"

The backup lights ignited. Sophia's long, sleek body with accentuated curves slid out of the garage. Joan peaked in the passenger window. Maretta sat there with a satisfied look on her face; a hand on the wheel while the other dialed the radio. Joan tossed her bag in the backseat and got in.

"What the hell do kids listen to these days?"

"Oh, I'm sure our parents asked the same thing when we were kids," Joan answered as she clipped her seatbelt on.

"Maybe," Maretta said as she settled on an oldies station.

"You know, I didn't even think to ask where we are going," Joan chuckled. Relief began to set in, the decision to go actually made.

"Not sure, wherever the wind takes us," Maretta backed out of the driveway, barely missing the mailbox.

* * *

California felt different. From the moment Glen felt the jolt of the plane hitting the runway two days ago he sensed the change. The streets were still lined with palm trees, and the stable sunny, seventy-something weather was the same, but it was as if Glen returned home with different eyes. Gone was the top-of-the-world high he felt living here, in one of the most coveted cities.

"You look like you just lost your best friend," the taxi driver said briefly turning his head to look back at Glen.

Glen didn't answer, instead turned his head to look out the window, the driver's comment stabbing him in the heart. The driver changed the radio station to one that played softer tunes.

The traffic was light for an early Saturday morning. The taxi pulled up in front of Glen's office, a tall building that looked like it was made solely from glass. He handed the driver a fifty and told him to keep the change.

Glen looked down at the floor as he passed the security guard, briefly flashing him his id. The elevator doors opened immediately when he hit the up button and he was surprised at how grateful he was for that simple bit of luck.

Inside his office, he heaved his briefcase onto his desk chair. He opened it and fished out a few pictures that he had pulled off the memory boards posted at the funeral reception. Slowly, he flipped through them slowly for the fifth time today — he and his dad polishing Sofia, and one of his five-year-old self, handing his dad a wrench. The fishing trip picture of his Dad, brother and himself reminded him of his father making fun of them while they tried to take their catch off the hook. There was only one and the four of them — his mom, dad, brother and himself, in a rare formal pose, taken at a friend's wedding. He lined them up, one by one along the back of his desk next to the only framed photograph already there.

I'm such an ass, he thought to himself. He walked over and leaned his head against one of the floor to ceiling windows in his corner office. When the skin on his forehead started to feel like it was sizzling bacon, he left it there, thinking he deserved the punishment as he reflected on his behavior.

"I think you got us out of the house just in time," Glen said as Paul made a right turn.

"Yea," Andy leaned forward from the back seat. "If we stayed, Mom would have broke out in to her 'When are you going to grow up and have kids like Paul' rant."

"Don't be in any hurry guys," Paul answered as he glimpsed at Andy in the rearview mirror. "Don't get me wrong, I love Julie and my kids, wouldn't trade em for the world, but it's a lot of work and expensive!"

"Someday," Glen murmured. "Maybe."

"Hey, it's not like I wouldn't like to have some mini mes. But, trying to find a girl who gets my lifestyle isn't easy," Andy confided.

They drove in silence the rest of the way, each in their own thoughts. As they neared their old stomping grounds, they noticed the old wood carved sign was replaced with a modern, engraved metal plated one. The newly paved parking lot was packed.

"Wow, this place is happening," Andy said as they searched for a space.

"*Wonder who we'll run into,*" Glen sat upright and smoothed his hair back.

What an ass, Glen repeated to himself. *Who did we run into?* A bunch of carefree, college-age kids, and a few he was sure got into their beloved bar with fake id's. They couldn't even finish a beer. They felt like a bunch of dirty old men.

On the streets below, crowds gathered on each corner, waiting to cross — moms with strollers, lovers holding hands, joggers running in place. *Normal people*, he thought, *normal people living life, having a life, not spending it alone in an office on a Saturday. I need to make some changes in my life, big changes.*

Chapter 4

It was easy for them to agree which direction to head.

"South, much more to see," Maretta said when they hit the end of Maple Way.

"I agree, take a left. We'll need to get on I-95. I'll show you how," Joan pointed towards the road that would lead them straight through the center of town first.

Maretta followed Joan's instructions.

They entered their sleepy, little, one-block hometown in upper New York State. One-story buildings, made of various materials, lined both sides of the Main Street. Suddenly, Joan coward into her seat.

"Duck!" she said.

"Duck? How the hell am I supposed to drive?" Maretta turned and looked at her friend with her eyebrows wrinkled. "What are you trying to hide from?"

"Tom Kisco, don't you see him coming out of the coffee shop on the corner. If he sees us, our secret will be out," Joan scrunched like a pretzel below the dashboard. "Who cares." Maretta beeped and waved at Tom who nearly spilled his coffee onto his chest. "Too late."

Maretta sat up straighter and took a quick peek at Tom in the rearview mirror. He stood there waving his free arm in the air at them frantically. "Words out now."

Joan uncoiled and turned around to see Tom's reaction for herself. "The whole town will know."

"I wish you had seen his face when he saw Charlie's car and then squinted to see who was driving it."

"There," Joan interrupted and pointed, "get on the highway just ahead."

Maretta pulled the car over onto the shoulder. "Let's put the top down first. Maretta reached over and before Joan could reject, the trunk door was lifting like a dump truck and the vanilla-colored-vinyl top lifted above their heads, folded like a neatly stacked pile of laundry, and tucked itself into the trunk. The old granny smell was replaced with fresh, cool morning air.

"We're off," Joan announced raising her fist in the air, feeling rejuvenated. "Did the boys give you any flack for taking the car?"

"No," Maretta said as a Cheshire cat smile snuck on her face. She merged onto the highway.

"You didn't?" Joan asked knowing full well what the answer was.

"Why invite trouble? I didn't even tell them I was leaving."

Joan laughed as she confessed, "I didn't tell Paul either!"

A trucker slowed down in the lane next to them and ogled at the car. Maretta looked at him as she gripped the steering wheel tighter with both hands. He gave her the thumbs up and mouthed, "Nice car."

Maretta mouthed *thank you* and flicked her head forward for him to move on. He got the message and left them behind.

"We may end up attracting more attention than we know what to do with in this car," Joan said.

"We deserve it," Maretta said and pressed a little harder on the gas pedal.

They cruised in silence down Interstate 684. The sun warmed the left side of their faces. The trees in Westchester County, New York were fully leaved and the pace of early summer could be felt. It was several miles before Maretta noticed they were running low on gas. "Shit, I should have checked that before we left."

"Don't worry, get off at the Armonk exit, it's coming up in just a couple miles."

Maretta looked at the gas gauge again and nodded. After the umpteenth car passed them slowly, she chuckled, "I haven't been gawked at so much since before I married Charlie."

"Too bad it's the car," Joan replied.

Maretta smiled as her thoughts floated back to the first time she road in the car with her Charlie.

"Want a ride?" Charlie asked as he pulled the brand new 1963 Ford Thunderbird up to the curb where she stood.

School had just let out and all the kids turned to look at

the car. Maretta held her books to her chest as her insides fluttered but she tried to remain cool. She hesitated for a minute;
she didn't really know Charlie Goodall. He wasn't in school
much, always out helping his Dad run his plumbing business.

"Where you off to?" he inquired.

"I'm meeting my friends at the soda shop." She reached up
with her right hand and ran her fingers through her curly,
shoulder length, blond hair. It was a brilliant, sunny May
afternoon. She could easily walk the three blocks to town.

"Hop in, I'll drive you," he waved her closer.

Maretta tilted her head to see who was watching. Everyone. "Okay."

"There, exit 3, get off there," Joan pulled Maretta back
into the present. The gas station isn't far off the exit.

* * *

"Are you sure you can drive over the George Washington
bridge?" Joan shouted through the wind. "Do you want me
to drive?"

"I've driven over a bridge before," Maretta shouted back,
not taking her eyes off the right lane of interstate 87. There
was a lot of traffic on the road. Cars, vans, motorcycles and
tractor trailers whizzed by them in the other two lanes,
occasionally darting into her lane to avoid potholes. *How
do people commute into New York City every morning like
this? I would get a stomach ulcer,* Maretta wondered.

Joan drew a deep breath in and held it. She took another

peak at the speedometer, pretending to be looking at traffic. Forty-five miles per hour, no wonder they were getting honked at and people were giving them the finger. It had been years since she had driven over the GW Bridge. Getting on I-95 was the quickest way to get south.

"Okay, then you need to get off at the next exit, 7S." Joan pointed at the sign ahead.

Maretta nodded in agreement and grabbed the steering wheel tighter, not daring to let go, except to turn the blinker on. As the exit approached, she eased off, staying in the right lane.

"Now you have to get in the left lane, "Joan announced while she looked behind them to see if there was an opening. "Quickly," she added.

Without looking Maretta turned the wheel to the left. A car behind honked without letting up. Maretta jerked the car back into the right lane. Her nerves sizzled.

"Not yet!" Joan shouted as the car passed by them. "Now! Hurry!"

Maretta flicked her head back this time, saw a narrow opening in the line of cars and floored it.

Joans body heaved forward, "Slow down, this is a sharp turn!"

The centrifugal force pinned Joan against the door and Maretta's torso was heading closer as the wheels squealed against the pavement. Yellow signs with black arrows raced by their eyes. Caught in the web of roads and bridges that intertwined, they had no choice but to hold on and go forward. The road took them higher and higher, the exit ramp way below them. It was as if they were on a terrifying roller-coaster ride.

Maretta tasted blood in her mouth, but could only lick it away from where she had bit deep into her lip. She traded the gas pedal for the brake, their heads lunged forward, then back like ragdolls.

"You can't stop!" Joan screeched. *Maybe I should have had a glass of wine before we left,* she thought. *And I thought teaching Paul how to drive as a teenager was bad.*

Maretta went back to the gas, and by some miracle eased her way into the hectic pace of the traffic on I-95. Her confidence rebooted. But that didn't last long.

"There will be a lot of signs and road choices up ahead," Joan tried to warn. "There is an upper deck and lower deck to the bridge."

"I'm trying to concentrate," Maretta barked back. A tractor-trailer nudged in front of her, blinding her from seeing the traffic signs. By the time she saw them, they were blurry streams of green and white passing overhead. She swerved to the left; the car behind them screeched his brakes. Maretta could see another row of the green and white signs now but it was like trying to read the menu behind the counter at McDonalds while going 50 miles per hour.

"Which way do I go?" Maretta screamed.

Joan was frozen. This bridge always terrified her, but when she was driving at least she was in control. Her right foot was going numb pretending to press on a brake that wasn't there. She stared straight ahead, dazed.

A souped-up, low-riding Mazda darted in front of them. As soon as Maretta slammed on the brakes, he whizzed across two more lanes as swift as a hummingbird. "Shit!"

More signs flashed overhead.

"Which way?" Maretta begged as she reached over and whacked Joan's left arm with her hand.

Joan snapped out of her panicked state and looked up. "Move over to the middle lane," she answered and hoped they would end up in one of the lanes heading over the bridge. *God help us*, she thought, *if we miss the bridge and end up in the Bronx*.

Maretta slowed the car, which only provoked those behind her to pass on the right and the left.

"Come on," she mumbled to herself as she looked for an opening in her side mirror. "Someone let me in."

Joan looked straight ahead and prayed. The car made a sharp shift and they were in the middle lane. Darkness engulfed them as they headed through tunnels, lights whizzing past them overhead. The smells of exhaust making them choke. Then, in one glorious moment, they were blinded by daylight. Steel grey towers stood resolute. They could have been mistaken for Superman and Batman standing with their arms crossed, chests puffed out and feet planted on the ground, guarding the entrance to New York City. The thickly wrapped cables suspending the roads resembled harp strings.

Joan made the sign of the cross as she whispered, 'Thank you, Lord."

Maretta allowed herself a quick glance to the left to see

the New York City skyline along the gleaming Hudson River. Joan stole a peak of the mighty Hudson River stretching to the north, stately rock walls lining one side, rows of towns the other. A tugboat chugged along the center.

"We did it!" Maretta reached a fist up in the air and let blood flow again in the fingers of the other.

Joan's right foot let off of the imaginary brake. She shifted herself in her seat and looked over at her friend. "You're bleeding."

Maretta's neck stretched so she could see herself in the rearview mirror. Blood dripped from her bottom right lip. "Do you have a tissue?"

Joan sifted through her purse, pulled out a tissue, and dabbed it on her friend's lip. "You pay attention to the road. We're not done yet."

The maze of roads entering New Jersey took them through a series of harrowing turns and exits before finally dumping them onto the New Jersey Turnpike. "The New Jersey Turnpike is the same thing as I-95," Joan said.

"Where the hell is the sign that tells you that?" Maretta said frustrated. Shooting pains began to fire down the right side of her neck. Doubt began to creep in. *Maybe I have bit off more than I could chew.* She did a quick coin toss in her mind, turn around and go back or keep going. *I don't have enough strength to get back over that bridge right now. Besides what would I be going home to? No,* she decided, *keep going.* Besides, she didn't want to admit defeat or weakening to Joan.

Joan coached Maretta through the next series of merges. The sun got hotter as it rose above the new One World Tower in the far distance. They passed what looked like swamps filled with swaying reed grasses, The Met Life Stadium, and jet planes lifting off to various destinations as they passed Newark airport.

Maybe we should just grab a plane, Joan thought, and then realized, *to go to where?*

The scenery was unexciting, industrial. Bridges, each uniquely constructed, carried travelers to their destinations ahead. Sturdy power lines paralleled the highway. Billboards dotted the landscape promoting soft drinks, superior light beer and ways to get a whiter smile. The traffic lessened, and they fell into the traffic flow like a leaf floating atop a river.

Beep, Beep! "Nice car!" a man shouted from his BMW with his thumbs up.

Maretta smiled and waved.

Stacks and stacks of shipping containers lined up in parking lots near the highway and cranes, as tall as skyscrapers, stood ready to sort them. Maretta thought of her boys when they were young, playing with their Tonka toys.

"The shipping industry is going to be big business someday," Charlie used to tell them. Charlie was a smart man and a good talker, an even better listener. He may not have had a college degree, but he used his people skills to his advantage; getting stock tips and business deals with some of his better-connected, well-off clients. He was everyone's favorite plumber, never had to advertise. All his work came word of mouth. Maretta never knew exactly what he was up to with their savings, but she trusted him and that paid off. He left her in a very good position financially.

"You won't have to work a day in your life," their accountant told Maretta after the funeral. "Go travel the world if you like, you'll have plenty of money left over."

It was a bittersweet revelation. All the years they lived a simple life; wearing the same three of four outfits over and over, homemade meals, an occasional vacation to Cape Cod, Massachusetts. This car was Charlie's biggest luxury. His one prized possession.

Joan pulled her shirt up over her nose as they neared exit 13.

"Yuck!" Maretta did the same. "What is that smell?"

Huge plumes of steam gushed from multiple steel chimneys on both sides of the highway. Three-story, round holding tanks bunched near the smoke stacks.

"Hold your breath," Joan warned Maretta, as she added, "Oil refineries."

Maretta tried to hold her breath, but began to feel a bit woozy. Instead she took slow shallow breaths and began to wonder if she should pull over and put the top back up.

"This is why they call New Jersey the armpit of the nation," Joan shouted.

"They need to invest in some deodorant," Maretta replied. "How the hell did they ever get named 'The Garden State'?"

"We need to go further south or west to see that part."

When the smell of rotten eggs, mixed with fuel, began to wane, they each slowly pulled their shirts off their faces. They let their noses sniff around the new air. Up ahead, a welcome sight, Thomas Edison Rest Area.

"I'm going to pull off," Maretta announced.

Joan shook her head in agreement. *I need to get off this roller coaster ride.* She began to wiggle her legs, hoping they would still hold her up.

Maretta turned the car off the exit, missed the turn off for cars and found herself with no choice but to park in the tractor-trailer section. She shifted into park; let out a huge sigh and let her head fall back onto the headrest. Her eyes closed.

Joan placed both her hands on her face, then let them rake through her hair and massaged the back of her neck with her fingers.

"I thought we were going to die," Maretta confessed. "Now I know how a sock in a washing machine feels."

Joan remained silent.

Maretta opened her eyes, gazed at the white, fluffy cloud inching its way across the clear blue sky. Her shoulders released their grasp from her ears. She turned to look at Joan. She started to chuckle at first, as she reached her hand up to her mouth.

"What?" Joan looked at her inquisitively.

Maretta began to laugh. Her hand reached for her belly as she bent over and tears began to stream down her face as she gasped for a breath. She tried to stop so she could share with Joan what was making her laugh, but the more she tried, the harder she laughed.

"What?" this time Joan asked more eagerly.

Maretta gasped, then dove back into hysterics. She gasped again, as if she were frantically trying to prevent herself from drowning, and pointed her finger at Joan's head. "Your," was the only word she could get out before another wave of laughter engulfed her. After her next inhale, she forced out the words, "your hair!"

Joan's brow's relaxed and she turned to look in the mirror. Her soft, mature grey curls had unfurled leaving her with half-hazard strands sprouting from her head. A giggle bubbled up inside, and her body began to quiver. She looked over to Maretta. The giggles rose to a boil as their laughter entrained.

Joan pointed at Maretta, she too gasped for air, "Look at you!"

Maretta, out of breath, took some slow deep inhales then stretched her neck to look in the rearview mirror. Her hair, once a neat flat bob, now jetted straight back like a rock-n-roll star. Her bottom lip was beginning to puff out. "We look like we lived through a tornado."

With that they both grabbed their stomachs and laughed so hard they didn't even notice the large bus pull up next to them.

Chapter 5

The bus hissed and its door opened. One by one an army of men, all different nationalities, marched out dressed in jeans and t-shirts. One of the men, tall, muscular, with skin the color of leather left the group and wandered over to Sophia. He peeled his sunglasses off, stood at the front and gently touched the hood.

The ladies began to recover from their fit of laughter, wiping away their tears and sighing. The man bent over and look under the front of the car, and then traced his finger gently along the side until he was standing over Maretta, blocking the sun.

"Beautiful car," he said with a Hispanic accent.

"Thank you," Maretta answered, while Joan desperately tried to tame her locks.

"1963?" he asked.

"Yes, are you a collector?" Maretta asked. She opened the door and stood. Her eyes met his sculpted chest.

"No, in my country we have lots of vintage cars," he answered. "My grandmother would never drive like you ladies are."

"Are you calling us old?' Joan chimed in placing her hands firmly on her hips.

"No, no, not at all! This car make you two look like teen-agers," he smiled showing off a perfect set of snow-white teeth. His dark eyes sparkled.

"See, Joan, this road trip is going to be our fountain of youth," Maretta said as she turned to her friend then back to the dashing young man. "Where is your country?"

"Cuba," he answered.

"Are you on an adventure too?" Joan asked looking at the tour bus.

"No, I play baseball, we are headed to our next game."

"Hey, Romeo, we are going to be leaving soon," one of the guys shouted as they began to get back on the bus.

"Do you mind if I get a picture of us to share with my friends?" He asked. "Do you tweet or do Facebook?"

Maretta and Joan looked at each other, and shrugged their shoulders. Joan got out of the car.

"No," Joan answered him proudly, "we text."

The man tilted his head in confusion, "Oh, okay, that's good. Any communication is good. My name is Alejandro by the way."

"Maretta," she reached out her hand to his and shook it, "my friend, Joan."

Joan nodded.

"Reggie, can you get a picture of us?" Alejandro asked.

The three posed with giant smiles, the ladies on either side with an arm wrapped around Alejandro's waist.

"Make sure you get the car in too," he insisted.

"We need one too," Joan handed her phone to Reggie. "We need to text a picture to our friends."

After the last shot, Alejandro looked at the picture on his phone and began to type. *Check out this awesome car these #CoolGrannies are driving!* He hit tweet.

"It's been a real pleasure to meet you two." His smile made them swoon. They exchanged gentle hugs.

"You too, Alejandro."

"Last call!" the bus driver shouted out the window.

"Go to go. Drive safe," and he was gone.

Joan went inside to use the rest stop bathroom while Maretta topped of the gas. She scurried in to the gift shop lined with magazines, books, miniature toiletries and treats along the walls. In the center was a table of neatly stacked t-shirts, a mannequin wearing one, in the center.

"Do you sell scarves?" Joan asked the young woman behind the counter who was focusing on her cell phone.

"Scarves?" the girl asked peeking up to respond to Joan.

"Yes, you know, the kind you wrap around your neck or can tie in your hair?" Joan began to pace nervously. That last thing she needed was to keep Maretta waiting too long and have her start to get bitchy.

"I don't think so," the woman said as she returned her attention to the phone.

"This store is the size of my kitchen and you don't know what's in it?" Joan muttered under her breath as she walked around the store one more time knowing her hunt was fruitless. She stopped at the table, picked up a hot pink t-shirt with an image of New Jersey across the front and *The Garden State* written along the bottom.

"I'll take this," she said as she dropped it on the counter and hastily scoured through her purse for money. "Do you have a scissor?"

"A scissor?" the woman asked.

Annoyance began to seep through Joan's pores as she began to wonder if this woman was mocking her or just utterly clueless. "Yes, a scissor," she replied as she held her hand up and clapped her pointer and middle finger together.

The woman reached under the counter, retrieved a scissor and handed it to Joan. Joan spread the t-shirt flat on the counter and filleted it open while the woman watched with raised eyebrows. Joan cut the t-shirt in a triangle, gathered her hair and smoothed it back, then wrapped the t-shirt around her head like a bandana. The bewildered woman handed Joan her change.

That's one hell of a car," the gas attendant let his eyes saunter along the light beige vinyl interior, stopping to admire the dashboard.

"Thank you," Maretta replied.

"Gosh, metal flip top ashtrays in the doors, remember those? Mind if I take a picture?"

"Go ahead," Maretta shrugged.

Joan opened the passenger door as the attendant snapped pictures.

"You've got to be kidding," Maretta gasped.

"It's better than looking like I put my finger in a socket," Joan replied. "What's with the picture taking?"

"Don't let your head swell," Maretta said as she posed with her hand behind her head.

"I know, it's the car," Joan joked. She didn't share how much she ached for some attention — a hug to greet the day, someone to tell her she was beautiful, tuck her hair lovingly behind her ear. Maretta would find that out herself, in due time. It had been so many years since her husband died, the shock of the call, long worn off now.

"Joan, your husband," the neighbor's voice quivered. "He tipped over in his tractor, on the hill."

It was Charlie who came and picked Joan up from the nursing home where she worked. It was Charlie who confirmed the body. It was Charlie and Maretta who took her and Paul into their family and never let them go.

I owe Maretta, Joan thought.

The pair returned to the New Jersey Turnpike.

The gas attendant opened his twitter app to post one of the pictures. There on his feed was Alejandro's post.

"Hey guys, he called out to his co-workers. Look, Alejandro Lorenz, the major league baseball player, was just here posing with those ladies in that dope car." While his colleagues huddled around him to see his phone, he tweeted his picture, "I found the #CoolGrannies too!"

Chapter 6

The exhilarating sensation between Connie's thighs had ceased long ago, but she waited patiently for Harold to climax. *I don't remember my husband going on for this long,* she thought to herself. She studied the pattern on the drawn curtains, noticed a spider crawling along the ceiling, until finally he let out a loud moan that sounded more like the moo of a hungry cow. He rolled off of her and lay flat on his back, repositioning the pillow under his head.

"That was good," he sighed.

"Mmm, hmm," Connie hummed as she reached into her bedside table drawer and pulled out a pack of cigarettes and a lighter. The package crinkled as she pulled the plastic wrapper off and then flipped the lid open. She let the sweet tobacco aroma of her teenage years take her back in time. She selected a single cigarette, withdrew it, placed it into her mouth and let her lips purse around it. The lighter's flame danced on the other end, she sucked in deeply. Slowly, she withdrew the cigarette held between her two fingers, let her breathe be still, and then tilted her head towards the ceiling, letting the smoke escape.

Harold opened his eyes and promptly propped himself up on his elbow as he thrust frustration towards her, "What are you doing?"

"Smoking," Connie answered nonchalantly, then returned the cigarette to her waiting lips.

"I didn't know you smoked," Harold said.

The lit end of the cigarette glowed a fiery red as she took another deep drag. Again, she let the smoke smother her mouth and lungs as long as she could, before exhaling.

"I don't," she reached over, pulled an ashtray from the drawer and let the cigarette rest in one of its grooves. "Only after sex. Want one?"

"Only after sex? You're just telling me this now?" Harold huffed, kicked the sheets off and sat on the side of the bed. He stood up and headed straight for the chair where he had thrown his clothes and began to get dressed.

Connie wasn't about to let him steal her joy. She lavishly reached over for the cigarette, which was sending her inviting smoke signals. She took another puff.

"I've got to go," he said while he tucked his belt into a pant loop. "Dinner at six? I'll pick you up."

"See you then," Connie replied dreamily as he shut the door hard behind him.

The air actually felt lighter after he left. She indulged in the cigarette for several minutes before squishing the remains into the ashtray. She picked up the new iPhone her daughter bought her yesterday, hoping there might be a message from the travelers. She punched in her code and watched all the different colored squares appear. She felt overwhelmed, like she just landed on another planet.

"Why do I need one of these?" she asked her daughter. It had taken Connie so long to figure out and get comfortable with the flip phone.

"Mom, you need to upgrade. Your phone is so old. There are so many other things you can do with a phone today."

"Like what?" Joan retorted.

"Check the weather, take pictures and videos, get directions-lots of things."

Reluctantly, Connie gave in to her youngest daughter. Somehow she sensed that there was more to this. She noticed how her daughters never talked to each other on their phones anymore but interacted via their phones constantly.

Lounging in her bed, her back against the headboard, she tapped the weather app. *Partly cloudy, chance of rain. I'll wear my pantsuit tonight instead of my pink dress.*

Then she tapped the box with a camera on it. She tapped on the screen, and a picture of her kitchen sink came up. It was the only photo on her phone. Her daughter took it yesterday when she demonstrated how to use the camera feature. *I don't want this on my phone,* Connie thought frustrated. She tapped it once, twice, it got bigger, went away, came back. She tapped at the screen harder, faster.

"Hello?" a groggy voice asked from the phone.

Connie looked closer. "Stacy?"

"Mom?" her youngest daughters image grew bigger in the screen.

"Stacy?" she repeated.

"Mom, you are face timing me," she rolled her eyes, looked behind her, then back at the screen. It's 9:30 a.m., on a Saturday. My only day to sleep in." She rubbed her eyes.

Connie's hands relaxed and her phone tilted forward. "I'm sorry," she began.

"Mom! I don't want to see your boobs! Put some clothes on," Stacy insisted.

"Oh my God, how can you be seeing my breasts?" Connie asked. She sat up straighter.

"You have the screen tilted towards your chest."

Connie slammed the phone down on the table and pulled the blanket up to her chin. "Now what can you see?"

"The ceiling," Stacy said, her tone exasperated. "Listen, we are making some new phone rules: no calling before 11 a.m. unless it's an emergency and no face timing until we give you an in-service."

"You're the one who wanted me to get this," Connie said as she snickered to herself.

"I'm going back to bed. I'll talk to you later."

"But, how do I turn it off?"

Silence.

Connie reached over, slid the phone into the bedside drawer and closed it. *I don't want the whole town to see me.*

Just a few miles down the road, Ann stood at her kitchen sink letting warm water run over her hands, putting her into a trance-like state. She picked up the soapy frying pan and rhythmically scrubbed it with the scouring side of the sponge. Outside she watched as a squirrel jumped from branch to branch.

The outdoors is always changing, full of life, she thought. The tall maple trees blocking the morning sun shaded half of the backyard. The other half of the yard lit brightly, show-casing the newly planted geraniums, budding hydrangeas and flowering dogwood.

Maretta and Joan are out there, exploring, experiencing what life has to offer. She scrubbed the pan harder. *That used to be me. I used to be the one traveling on luxurious vacations-Paris, Amsterdam, the Caribbean.* She slammed the pan into the draining board.

Roland lifted his knife quietly, and eased it over to the stick of butter lying on the antique butter dish. He shaved a half-inch thick slice off. He kept one eye on his wife. He lathered the pat of softened butter gently onto his slice of already buttered whole-wheat toast. *Hell, ya gotta die of something. May as well enjoy yourself while you're here.* Indulgently he bit into the toast and let the creamy, some-what salty texture blend with the crunchy wheat.

He didn't dare interrupt Ann's thoughts until he popped the last bite into his mouth, savored it, then washed it down with a sip of steaming hot coffee. He noticed she hadn't been acting the same since her friends left town.

"Why didn't you go with them?"

Ann turned the running water off, wiped the rim of the sink with a dishtowel, and then turned to face her husband.

"Go with who?"

"Your friends — Maretta and Joan."

Ann gathered up her husband's dishes and returned to the sink. "Because they were being ridiculous. You don't just throw things in a bag, hop in the car and go traveling. At least not at this age."

Roland got up from the table, pushed his chair in and placed his used napkin on the counter next to Ann. "You are wound too tight," he said then kissed her on the head and headed for the door. "I'm off to the club."

"Stay away from those hot dogs, I am making a healthy broiled chicken dish tonight."

The door clicked shut. Ann listened as the garage door creaked open, the car engine started then the door creaked close again. She stood in the lifeless, silent kitchen and began polishing the sparkling granite counter tops. "I don't know why I bother."

The kitchen phone rang. Grateful for the distraction, she answered it, "Hello."

"Are you going to the garden club meeting today? I can pick you up," Connie asked.

Skipping right over her question, Ann asked, "Have you heard from them?"

"Maretta and Joan?"

"No, Laurel and Hardy," Ann ripped off her apron. "Yes, Maretta and Joan."

"No, not a word. You?" Connie realized after she asked

that the likelihood they would contact Ann before her was slim to none.

"No, I hope they are alright. Doesn't Joan have heart problems?"

"I'm sure they are fine. No news is good news."

Connie's cheeriness only made Ann more irate. "They really shouldn't be out there without a plan. What if their car breaks down in the middle of nowhere?"

"I guess they'll call a tow truck." Connie said paying more attention to the fly bashing his body against the window trying to get out.

Ann huffed into the phone. It was useless to discuss her concerns with the always ignorantly optimistic Connie. "Yes, I planned on going to the garden club meeting today. I can drive myself. I will see you there."

"Okay, see you there."

"Let me know if you hear anything," she said.

Chapter 7

Andy strummed his guitar, desperately trying to find the right chord, while his band mates took a break. The disharmonic energy hovered in the air. He knew he was the reason they weren't finding the magic today. The dimly lit room disguised the holes in the walls from more frustrating times. He felt lost.

His phone rang in his pocket and he willed himself to ignore it. Something inside, however, nudged him to answer it. When he saw his brother's name on the screen, he welcomed the diversion.

"Hey," Andy said as he lay his guitar down in his lap.

"Have you heard from Mom? I left a message for her yesterday and this morning, but she hasn't called me back," Glen asked.

"No," Andy answered, drawing in a deep breath. Family drama, just what he needed. Long ago Andy came to the conclusion that although he loved his brother deeply, if they weren't brothers, they probably would never be friends. "She's probably keeping herself busy."

"I'm beginning to worry."

The band members started returning to their instruments. They began tuning them. As the collision of sounds grew, it got difficult for Andy to hear.

"Listen, I'll give her a call after practice. We have a gig tonight and I'm not really feeling it."

"Yeah, I get that," Glen said somberly. "Okay, let me know if you hear anything and I'll do the same. Love you, bro."

Andy had to pull the phone away from his ear. He had to double check that it was his brother he was talking to. Love you, Bro? He put the phone back up to his ear and admitted, "Ya, love you too."

Feeling unsatisfied, Glen paced back and forth with the phone in his hand. Something just didn't feel right. For the first time, he felt anxious being so far away. When his Dad was here, he felt confident everything was being taken care of. Their safety net, their rock, was gone. The void made his knees weak, forced him to sit on the couch and bury his face in his hands.

The unknowing was rotting his insides. He dialed his phone again.

"Hey, Glen," Paul answered.

Glen got right to the point. "Paul, have you happened to see my mother around town?"

"No, why?"

"I've left her several messages but haven't gotten an answer."

"Tell you what, I'll give my Mom a call, she'll probably know where she is."

Glen felt bad asking his friend to keep an eye on his mom. He knew Paul already had enough on his plate. It was his responsibility. "I'd really appreciate it."

* * *

As soon as Joan saw the sign ahead, her gut clenched. Atlantic City, Exit 3. She looked straight ahead, pretending not to see it.

"Atlantic City!" Maretta pointed. "I have always wanted to go to a casino."

Joan tried to look on the bright side. At least they would stop, get out of the car. Maybe it would be enough to satisfy Maretta and they could go back home. The further they drove, the more uncertain Joan became. She looked at her friend but said nothing.

"I'm going to get off," Maretta said with a big smile. She began to sing a tune, something about feeling lucky.

As they neared Atlantic City, the expressway was lined with billboards of entertainment choices; shows, concerts, restaurants. Hotels jutted toward the sky in the horizon.

Maretta began to chatter excitedly, "Charlie would never stop at the casinos in Connecticut when we would go to the Cape. 'I'm already a winner, I still have my fifty dollars in my wallet,'" she mocked in a deep voice. "I used to tell him there was more to do than gamble, but nope, he would just drive straight past the exit. Do you think we'll see Donald Trump?"

Joan rolled her eyes. "I sure hope not." She bit her tongue and didn't say anything more. The election nearly cost them their friendship until they finally agreed to disagree. "Maybe Charlie was right." Joan suggested thinking about the two hundred dollars in her wallet. "If we gamble all the money we brought, we'll have to go home."

"You don't have to worry, this is on me," Maretta could see the worry on Joan's face. At some point she knew she would have to confide in her friend about the windfall Charlie left behind.

"I can't let you do that," Joan replied.

"When I met with Charlie's lawyer, he told me that Charlie left some money specifically earmarked for me to go and have fun with," she added the little white lie hoping to convince Joan to relax and have fun. "Just go with it," she added. Her youngest son, Andy, was always saying that to Maretta. *He is such a carefree soul, the total opposite of his brother*, she thought.

"Which casino should we go to?" Maretta scanned the streets ahead lined with shops, filled with cars going every which way. The stoplight turned red giving them a welcomed pause.

"That one" Joan pointed to the tallest one she could see, hoping it's stature would make it easier to find.

"Sounds good to me" Maretta cheered.

The skin on their faces welcomed the cool shade offered by the hotel's portico. Joan let out a deep sigh of relief as they drove past the larger-than-life-sized butterflies flapping mechanical wings, perched on flowers the size of horses.

Gaudy was the first thought that entered Joan's mind as she gazed up at the tray ceiling lined with flashing lights.

Before they could stop the car, two tidy gentlemen in dark grey valet jackets were headed towards them.

"Welcome to Jersey's best casino. That is one hot car!" the man on Maretta's side said.

"Hey, are you the Cool Grannies I keep seeing on twitter?" the gentlemen on Joan's side asked with wide eyes. He pulled his phone out of his pocket while looking around the portico. "We're not supposed to be on our phone while we are working. But, you look like the ladies I keep seeing on my feed." He quickly tapped his phone screen, flicked it a few times and showed the image of them on the turnpike- Joan holding her bandana on her head with one hand and Maretta smiling and waving at the camera while driving.

"Yes, that's us," Maretta said as she drew in a deep breath, thrust her chin up and puffed her chest out.

"Awesome! That's so amazing that you met Alejandro Lorenz. He's has the best batting average in the National League right now."

"Will you be staying with us?" the valet asked.

Simultaneously, the ladies answered.

Joan, "No."

Maretta, "Yes."

"I told you, don't worry about the cost, it's on me. I've got it all covered," she whispered to Joan with tight lips.

Joan pasted on a smile as she clasped her hands together. She looked straight ahead where the sun shined onto the exit road. *This is ridiculous, I'm beginning to feel like a hostage, she thought.*

The chivalrous men opened the doors and offered a

hand to help the ladies out of the car. The stockier of the two wheeled over the brass luggage rack, "Is this your luggage?" He pointed to the back seat.

"Yes," Joan answered.

He reached in and retrieved the black suitcase and put it on the rack. Then stopped.

Maretta felt a tingling creep up the back of her neck and across her face. She cleared her throat, and then pointed at the laundry bag, "that's mine."

"Oh, yes, of course," he said stealing a quick glance at his colleague before hurling the linen bag onto the luggage rack. "That everything?"

Maretta shook her head affirmatively. She looked up at the ceiling. Then down at the pavement she stood on. Slowly she raised her head and stared at the car. The valet standing near her stood with his hand out, palm up. She tightened her grip on the key in her hand, pulled it up and nestled it on her chest.

They all stood, for what seemed like an hour, in silence, watching Maretta.

"You are going to be careful with her, right?" she said not letting Sophia out of her sight.

"Absolutely. No need to worry. I have a special spot for cars like yours. See that yellow Ferrari over there?" He reached out, gently wrapped his hand around Maretta's arm, and she slowly turned her head. "That car there is worth over two hundred thousand dollars. I'm going to park your baby right next to her."

Maretta watched as a man with freshly polished shoes

got out of the yellow car and stood next to a tall, bleach-blond woman wearing spiked red heels and Jackie O style sunglasses. Gingerly, Maretta reached out her hand with the key in it. As her hand met the valets she opened it, and shifted the key in between her two fingers as he reached over and held the other side of the key with his two fingers. "There is an extra tip in it for you if I get her back without a scratch."

He bowed, still holding his side of the key. "Not necessary, I treat all the cars in my care as if they were my own. I can see, though, that this car means a lot to you." He winked and Maretta let the key go. She felt her throat constrict. She willed the burning sensation in her eyes to go away.

"Can we get a picture with you ladies and the car before we bring you and your luggage inside?" the bellman asked.

"Yes," Maretta snapped back to herself. "Yes, of course."

They huddled together close, smacked big grins on their faces as the bell man reached his long arms out as far as he could, "Say cheese."

"Cheese," they chimed.

"My name is Rafeal, by the way, let me escort you inside."

Joan and Maretta followed behind as Rafeal led them through the hotel doors. Maretta paused and looked back at the car. The valet sat in the seat, put the key in the ignition, looked over at Maretta, gave her the thumbs up sign and slowly drove away.

Joan scrunched her nose tight; the smell of faux floral air freshener, trying to disguise the smell of cigarette smoke, overwhelmed her olfactory system.

Maretta, showed no signs of being offended by the odor.

Instead she looked up at star-studded ceiling two stories above them, her eyes widened, she clasped her hands together and announced, "I'm gonna be a winner."

"That's what we like to hear," Rafeal said as the elevator rose. "You two have become quite the social media celebrities."

Maretta and Joan looked at each other, lifted their shoulders a bit, then looked back at the bellman and gently smiled trying not to look as clueless as they felt. The elevator doors opened saving them from further embarrassment.

Rafael paused after they exited. He looked over at the desk across the lobby, the one with a large VIP sign over it, then over to the check in desk to the left of them. "VIP?" he asked Maretta.

Maretta followed the path his eyes had just wandered. Standing at the VIP desk were the yellow Ferrari couple. Next to them a pile of matching luggage with a designer's logo stamped all over them. "No, we don't want to make a scene," she answered. "We'll just check in over here."

"Welcome, do you have reservations?" the woman behind the desk asked pleasantly.

"No, we decided to come last minute. Will that be a problem?" Maretta answered.

"No, not at all. Would you like an ocean facing room?"

"Yes, please, and two separate beds," Maretta replied.

Joan dug her compact out of her purse as Maretta checked in. She opened it and peered into the mirror. Rafeal stood next to her fiddling around on his phone, glancing up every few seconds to see if he was being watched.

"Look," he held the phone up for Joan to see. On the

screen was the picture they just took by the car with, *These grannies are cool! #coolgrannies* written above it. "Our picture already got 12 likes and 4 retweets. People love you ladies!"

Joan cringed at the site of herself in that photo. Her lips were bleak, colorless. Thin, straw-like strands of hair poked out from all sides of the pink bandana. *He could have at least waited until I put some lipstick on.* She reached over and turned the phone for a better look. She stared at image, pulled his hand closer and still said nothing. Then she let go of his hand, her eyes still staring towards the phone.

His words replayed again in her head, *Our picture already got 12 likes and 4 retweets. People love you ladies!"*

Just how many people did he share this picture with? Joan began to wonder. "So, is this like texting? You sent that picture to your friends?" She studied his face.

"Umm, yeah, I guess you could say it is like that," he tucked the phone back into the pocket of his jacket, nodding his head.

Deep in her gut, Joan felt something stir. Just what was all the fuss about with them, the pictures, and the car.

"Room 1021, Rafeal," the clerk announced as she held out a key card.

Maretta thanked the desk clerk, turned and noticed the bleach-blond woman heading towards the elevator. "Do you have a salon?"

"Yes, would you like me to book you an appointment?" the clerk responded.

"Yes," Maretta cast a quick glance at Joan, "two, we'll need two appointments. As soon as possible."

Chapter 8

The elevator doors opened invitingly. An elderly couple backed into the corner to allow them to enter.

"I still can't believe you chose red," Joan said. She stole a peak at her freshly coifed, golden-blond perm in the reflection of the stainless steel wall. She reached up and patted the curls. For the first time in years she actually felt younger.

"I love it," Maretta said. She, too, looked into the silvery walls at her reflection. "I've always wanted to try being a red-head." She leaned closer towards the wall and turned her head back and forth.

"Excuse me for eavesdropping," the plump woman behind them interrupted. "I just want to say, you ladies look dashing! We should spruce ourselves up at our age, we deserve it."

The man standing next to her rolled his eyes.

"Do you like these glasses?" the woman continued. She raised her hand up and held the arm of teal, blue-rimmed glasses with diamond studs running along the sides. She leaned closer to Joan and Maretta and said in a softer voice, "and I don't even need glasses, except for reading. They are my cheery glasses. They make me feel so happy! I have them in six different colors. These highlight my blue eyes." She opened her eyes wider.

"Those are fun," Maretta confirmed. "Where did you get them, here?"

"Yes, in the shopping mall just down the boardwalk. The second or third store on the right, you can't miss them. They have a whole display in the window."

Their legs wobbled as the elevator slowed. The conversation stalled, the doors opened wide. The lobby was darker now. Fountains thrust water towards the ceiling. Swarms of people gawked at the enormity of the lobby. Their murmuring discussions blended into an indiscernible conversation.

Maretta tapped Joan on the elbow, "we may need to go and get some cheery glasses."

"Oh, I hope you do, they are so fun," the woman added. They merged into the crowd. "Have fun. Come on Harvey."

"You too," Maretta waved goodbye. "Shall we shop more or gamble?"

Maretta looked like a kid at an amusement park. She began bouncing onto her toes while looking back and forth, back and forth.

Joan weighed the options in her head. She wasn't sure more shopping was the right answer. They were already adorned with new outfits and had back ups in their room. Maretta glistened in a short-sleeved, white sweater, with three palm-sized glitter roses growing on the front of it. She lucked out getting the last petite sized, elastic waist pants that matched it. Joan talked her out of the Wizard of Oz ruby slippers that the sales lady really was pushing. "Get the black patent leather flats," Joan had argued. "They will go with more outfits and you don't want your feet to hurt from those heels."

Maretta eventually caved in to Joan's recommendation. When they got to the salon, however, Joan had no influence on Maretta's need to have auburn-red hair like Ginger Rogers had back in the day. The transformation from her part grey, part blond, bob hair made her almost unrecognizable.

"Let's gamble first," Joan picked, hoping it would be the less of two monetary evils.

"Gambling we go," Maretta bolted towards the flashing lights and dinging sounds in the distance.

"Would you like a cocktail?" the waitress asked Maretta as she leaned over and placed a cocktail napkin next to the slot machine.

"It's a little early for that, isn't it?" Maretta replied looking up at her.

"They're free, go ahead, have one, you know what they say, 'It's 5 o'clock somewhere,'" the woman sitting at the slot machine to the left of Maretta teased as she raised her half-filled plastic cup.

"Free?" Maretta questioned, looked over her shoulder at Joan who was pulling the leaver so slowly you would think she was afraid she was going to break it.

"Yeah, free. They figure if they get you sloshed you'll

gamble more." The woman took another sip of the golden liquid, then reached up, wrapped her hand around the black knob at the end of the silver stick and yanked it down hard, "Come on diamonds!"

"I'll have a whiskey sour," Maretta said as she turned back to Joan and shouted over the dinging and ringing, "What do you want to drink?"

"Drink?" Joan replied just noticing the waitress.

"Yes, drink, and not water, a real drink, they're free."

Joan turned her attention back to the slot machine and watched as the three spinning blurs on the screen slowed-diamond, cherry, joker — another big fat zero in the moneybox. Her heart began to beat faster and she had a sudden urge to pee. "I'm fine for now," she said as she got up and raced towards the restrooms.

"Bring her one too, "Maretta instructed the waitress telling herself if Joan wouldn't drink it, she would.

Maretta and a collection of silver-haired and bald-headed people stopped to rubberneck as Joan watched the final diamond click into place beside the other two. The machine celebrated as if it was midnight on New Years Eve. The glowing numbers raced higher in the money window until they eventually stopped at four hundred and thirty-five dollars.

"You won again!"

As much as Joan tried to suppress it, a grin sprouted from her lips as she reached her hand up to cover it. *Oh, I wish my son were here to see this, she thought.*

"Well, that's it for me." The woman sitting to the right of Joan chugged down the last bit of her drink and stood up. "Guess it's not my lucky day. Congratulations." She gathered up her belongings, and looked down at her watch. "Boy, I forgot how you lose track of time in these places."

"Why, what time is it?" Joan asked thinking about the several ups, downs and near total losses she encountered since sitting in this seat.

"Eight o'clock," the woman replied nonchalantly.

"Eight o'clock," Joan gasped. She noticed that her stomach was growling. She said to Maretta, "Did you hear that? It is eight o'clock already."

"Eight o'clock, smeight o'clock," Maretta slurred.

"Come on, we need to get something to eat," Joan stood up as the waitress approached.

"Another whiskey sour?" she asked smiling.

Joan flattened her hand and raised it to her throat, rapidly flicking it back and forth as if she were sawing it off and shook her head no.

"Sure," Maretta replied, her glossy eyes meandering to meet the waitress's.

"No, we are fine, we are going to take a break," Joan interjected. "How do I get my money out of this thing?"

The waitress helped her get the payment ticket and pointed out the redemption windows, where she could trade it for cash.

Joan whispered to the waitress, "Maybe you could bring her some water?"

She nodded her head and left.

"Come on Maretta, let's cash you out too," Joan stood over Maretta's shoulder, and then reached to hit the appropriate button.

"No! I'm not ready. I'm here to win big," Maretta said like a bratty toddler. She slapped Joan's arm away, then caught herself before falling from her stool.

"Maretta, that is enough for today, we need to get out of here."

"You just want to go because you won. I'm not leaving here with," she stopped and leaned closer to the machine, her eyes squinting, "forty-three dollars." She let a pithy breath squeak out of her lips and reached for the lever again.

"I can't leave you here and I'm hungry. Let's get something to eat," Joan looked around for support but everyone around them was buried in the gambling zone. She wrapped her hand around Maretta's arm and firmly tugged at it to rise.

"I said no, I'm not going," Maretta's pitch rose and a few heads began to turn their way. Her arm flailed back and forth in Joan's tight grasp like a fish trying to get off a hook. Smack!

"Ouch, you hit me," Joan let go of Maretta's arm so she could tend to her jaw.

"Sorry bout that," Maretta slurred. "You won't listen to me. Go if you want, I'm staying. Waitress!"

Joan didn't know if she should yell or cry. Sure, they had their disagreements over the years, even had some silly alcohol induced moments, but she had never seen Maretta like this-a belligerent drunk. Softly she whispered, "Please, Maretta."

"I said no," Maretta screamed as she pulled the lever down with even more determination.

Joan stood behind Maretta for several minutes before announcing, "I'll be in the room." Without any feedback, she walked through the maze of machines, exchanged her ticket for cash, and then sought out the waitress. Handing the waitress a one hundred dollar bill, she pleaded, "Please generously water down any drinks my friend may order. She doesn't normally drink like this. We are in room 1021 if you need me. I can't get her to come with me."

The waitress tugged at the collar of her crisp, white-polyester shirt as she felt a thickness in her throat. This was the part of her job she hated, seeing old people turn into drunken bums. "I'll keep an eye out for her, but I can't promise anything."

"I understand," Joan replied gratefully.

Chapter 9

Maretta looked behind one shoulder, then the next, impatiently. *Where the hell is she?* She reached up for the slot machine lever, pulled it down as if she were holding on to the mast on a boat in stormy seas, and watched the screen. Nothing. She licked her lips. Again, she pulled the lever, this time nearly falling off her stool. Nothing. "Dammit," she said, smacking the screen.

The woman two seats down looked over. "You're out of money."

Sure enough, a big zero glowed in the cash window. Maretta held on to the machine as she willed her stiffened legs to rise. Her head began to swirl. She sat back down.

"I brought you some water," the waitress surprised her. She held out a cup and Maretta accepted it, then allowed the waitress to fill it to the top from a glass pitcher beading with sweat. "I'll leave this here, in case you want more."

"Thank you," Maretta wasn't going to argue. "Good idea." As she sat, allowing the ice-chilled fluid to purify her blood, she remembered her spat with Joan and immediately felt a pain in the back of her throat. *Ugg, I hope she doesn't hate me.* She guzzled down two more glasses of water before she attempted to get back up. The fog was beginning to clear, but she didn't dare take a step just yet. She sat back down, looked at the machine. "You took all my money. All my money is in there," she pointed. A fire began to simmer inside. She crossed her arms tightly as her teeth began to grind against each other making an audible crunching sound. Dinging, music pulsing, the sound of coins gushing like a waterfall enveloped her. "You took my money," she said again, this time louder, her finger authoritatively tapping on the screen. She rummaged through her purse and found a dollar tucked in one of the side pockets. "I want my money back," she told the machine sternly as she let it suck the dollar out of her hand, "and I want more!"

Her roar drew attention. She stood up and with both hands grasped the handle and repeated," I want my money back!"

With all her might she yanked it hard then stood back with a slight stumble. She locked her eyes on to the three windows with blurry images swirling. Everyone within earshot watched along with her.

Diamond.

The second whirling image slowed. She watched as the diamond passed by. *Shit.* It came back around and locked into place. Diamond.

"Give me my money back!" Maretta shouted.

Her gambling neighbors began to rise from their seats and strain for a better view. Some inched closer.

Maretta threw her hands up to her mouth in a prayer position as she chanted, "Diamond, diamond, diamond."

The last icons teased-cherry, joker, diamond; around and around they went.

"Diamond," Maretta wished as hard as she could feeling fully awake now. Her arms flew to the sky as she watched the last diamond slow and click into place. The machine erupted with glee. A screaming siren sounded, lights of all colors blazed, the numbers in the cash window shot up like a rocket headed for space. Maretta may as well have been the queen in a hive, onlookers swarmed around her. The waitress fought her way through until she stood shoulder to shoulder with Maretta. She reached around her and hugged her close as they all watched the numbers sprint upwards.

$10,764.

"You won!" the waitress wrapped both arms around Maretta who stood frozen; her eyes wide open as a tingling sensation glittered all over her body.

"You won," the waitress repeated, as she stepped away and jumped up and down.

Maretta felt multiple hands touching her. The crowd cheered.

"Woo, hoo!"

"Congratulations!"

"You did it!"

Maretta scanned around, hoping to see Joan. She stood on her tippy toes trying to peer over the crowd.

"She went upstairs," the waitress told her solemnly.

Maretta began to fan her face with her hands. She let the

waitress hit the cash out button and usher her away from the crowd.

* * *

"Are you sure you wouldn't like us to have security escort you back to your room?" the woman behind the cashiers window asked.

Maretta stuffed the wad of cash into her worn, brown leather bag and forced the clip along the top to lock. "No, I'll be okay, thank you."

"Well, congratulations. I hope you have fun with your winnings," the woman smiled.

Maretta nodded, hiccupped, then walked away not really sure where she was going. She weaved through the casino past rows of slot machines, crap tables, roulette wheels and people gathered around a table playing cards. None of the options excited her. She found herself taking an escalator to the first floor and out to the boardwalk along the ocean. A wide stretch of sand separated her from the waves rolling in. The reflection of the sun setting to the west cast a glow on the never-ending horizon. *It's so peaceful*, Maretta thought.

She knew by now, from the loss of parents, friends, and her first child, who was a stillborn, that life doesn't stop because you're hurting. No, the season of loss had come back around just the way spring, summer, fall and winter rotated. Each loss was unique, but this one, even more so, since Charlie was part of her everyday. She alone would have to remember their lifetime of memories. She alone would wake up to an empty house, sleep in a bed by herself, and cook, for whom? As night crept into the sky, she felt her soul darken as well. Abruptly, she turned and walked in search of the shops the woman wearing cheery glasses told her about, before she broke down in tears.

The brightly lit windows filled with glamorous dresses, colorful candy that would tempt any five-year-old, and high-end bags from all the well-known designers lifted Maretta's spirit a bit. Shoes, sunglasses, and the cheery glasses were all staged to lure the tourists who came to treat themselves. Maretta stopped and eyed a matching set of designer luggage. A young couple; he dressed in a military uniform and she sipping an iced drink, stopped at the jewelry window beside her.

Maretta couldn't help but eavesdrop.

"Which one do you like?" the soldier asked as her wrapped his arm around her waist.

"Oooo," she gushed and tossed her long chocolate-brown hair over her shoulder. "They are all gorgeous. Look at the sparkle."

He bent over and kissed her tenderly on the head.

She stared mesmerized at the window, and then pointed, "that one is pretty."

"Would you like me to show you something?" a tall, wide-shouldered man in a suit came out of the store and asked.

Before the young man could reply, the woman answered, "we're looking at engagement rings."

"Come in, come in, we have some gorgeous engagement rings," the salesman insisted.

The brunette followed the salesman's lead, letting him escort her into the store as she handed the soldier her cup. He stood there, his gaze falling to the ground. He reached into his pocket, pulled out his wallet, and counted the bills.

The soldier didn't seem to notice Maretta watching them. He looked through the window and he watched the woman holding up her hand with a sparkling rock on her finger. She twisted her hand side to side. Her smile grew wider. She waved her beau inside eagerly. He shuffled his feet along, dumping the cup in the garbage near the entrance, before going into the store.

Maretta inched her way over to the jewelry store window. She watched as the salesman pulled out another ring and the woman slid it on her finger, held her hand up and watched the stone shimmer the way sunlight dances on water. Her shoulders scrunched, she looked over and said something to the soldier. His lips formed in a shape of a smile, but the skin around his eyes didn't move. When she turned away, he instantly closed his lips and reached a hand into the pocket where his wallet lay and held it there.

"I wish I could buy you a bigger diamond," Maretta remembered Charlie telling her as she reached up and wrapped her fingers around the heart pendant. "Someday I will. We'll go on a real honeymoon, too." It was as if she was nineteen-years-old again. The two of them, sitting on a red and white picnic blanket as the Katonah River flowed before them. Chirping birds sang, streaks of sun found their way through the new green leaves, and a hint of lilac danced in the breeze.

Maretta believed every word he said, as if his promises were written in stone. *Oh the life they would have together*, she remembered thinking. But, the bigger diamond never came, nor did a better honeymoon. After the wedding, they went to a cabin in the Adirondacks. Then life pushed all her young dreams aside and practicality moved in.

By the fourth ring, Maretta couldn't take it anymore. She watched as the soldier fiddled with his wallet in his pocket and his body began to wilt. She barged into the store. "Which one do you like the best?" she asked the young woman. The salesman took a step back.

"I'm sorry?" the young woman questioned, her eyebrows scrunched.

"I said, which one do you like best?" then she turned to the soldier and added, "you only get one chance to get engaged."

The young woman looked at the ring on her finger, then at the tantalizing choices that sat under the glass counter-top. "That one," she pointed, and then looked at the salesman, "the pear shaped one."

The salesman jumped behind the counter, reached in for the pear-shaped ring, exchanged it for the one on her finger. She slid it on. "I've always dreamed of having a pear-shaped diamond engagement ring."

Maretta walked closer, looked at her finger. "How much?"

The salesman pulled the velvet ring box out and looked underneath it. "$9500," he announced.

The couple drew in a deep breath as if the oxygen had just left the room. The soldiers face winced.

The young woman forced a weak smile on her face as she replied, "It's okay. Any ring will do." She leaned over and kissed her boyfriend on the lips then began to wiggle the ring off her finger.

The salesman stared hard at Maretta.

Maretta returned the stare and leaned closer to the counter. "She'll take it." She snatched the ring from the woman and handed it to the soldier. She could see Charlie in his military uniform, saluting her, in her minds eye. "You military guys are full of high hopes and promises that our government doesn't always support."

The soldier spoke, "Umm, we can't accept this."

"You don't have a choice," Maretta flicked open the latch on her purse and the cash burst out like a pair of double D breasts being unleashed from a push-up bra. "I want to do this. Think of it as a thank you gift for your service." She gathered the bundles of cash, and shoved it at the man. "Go ahead, count it, and let me know what the total is with tax. Unless, of course, you offer a special deal for cash." She looked over and winked at the couple standing there stunned.

Maretta left the jewelry store satisfied that she had just enough to buy that luggage she had eyed earlier. She turned to look back at the couple in the store. The soldier was down on his knees.

Chapter 10

Cheerios were strewn all over the kitchen floor. Julie stood at the stove scrambling eggs, dictating orders to the baby, sitting in the high chair. "Eat the cheerios, don't throw them," and "sit down, your eggs are almost ready," to the toddler.

Paul waved the white flag, long ago, after learning it was best to just wait until after they were done eating before trying to help clean up or just let the dog in. Saturday meant there would be a list on his honey do list: go with them to the farmer's market, stop at the park and let the boys burn off the energy from the muffins they ate, mow the lawn, and whatever else. He saw his wife's notepad on the table. Todays add ons looked long. He backed out of the kitchen before Julie could give him his marching orders. He wanted to try and call his Mom one more time.

"Mom, I'm starting to worry, where are you? Call me." He put the phone down on the coffee table. It was too early to call Glen.

* * *

Joan rubbed her eyes, then rolled over, stuffing the pillow deeper under her head. *That's funny, why is this pillow case so scratchy*, she wondered. The thought triggered her to open her eyes. She was greeted by the dawn's light streaming through the sheer curtains. It was unfamiliar territory-a stiff looking, grey-blue checkered chair in the corner, water-color paintings depicting ocean scenes and heavy, sea-blue drapes condensed to just a foot wide on either side of the window. Then it came to her. *I'm in Atlantic City.*

She shimmied her hips to the middle of the bed and eased her way onto her side. In the bed next to her, Maretta laid flat on her back, mouth wide open making intermittently gasping for breath sounds.

Joan's thoughts retreated to the voice mails she listened to on her phone last night.

"Hi Mom, just checking in, hope you are having a good day."

"Hi Mom, did you get my call? Call me back?"

"Mom, Glen called. Aunt Maretta isn't calling him back. Is she with you? Why aren't you returning my calls?"

Last night Joan wrestled with the thought of calling her son for hours. Those thoughts intermingled with wondering if she should go and try again to retrieve Maretta. To make matters worse, she realized she forgot the plug for her cell phone. Exhaustion eventually took over. She ended up doing neither.

Joan sat up and held the side of the bed with her hands

as she flexed her feet back and forth feeling the taut muscles resist.

Maretta gave out a sudden deep snort, then went into a fit of coughing, jarring her eyes open. She turned on her side, dug her elbow into the bed and pushed herself up to a sitting position. She continued to cough until her throat cleared. Joan got up, turned a light on and filled a glass of water from the tap and handed it to her, "Here, you might need this."

Maretta accepted it and sipped half of it down. Smacking her lips in gratitude.

"Did you win?" Joan asked in a deadpan tone.

"Yes, but I lost it all," Maretta said, reaching over to put the glass on the faux wood bedside table. "But, I got you a pair of cheery glasses." Maretta rummaged through the shopping bag next to her bed, pulled out a bright yellow pair of glasses and handed it to Joan.

An uncomfortable silence settled between them. Joan fondled the glasses in her hands.

How can I get her to agree to go back home? Joan mulled.

I shouldn't have drunk so much; Maretta concluded, a sharp throb in her brain reminding her of her indulgence last night. She reached over for the water glass and gulped down the rest. *Maybe we should leave Atlantic City today, continue on our adventure.*

"They're on to us," Joan announced.

"Who?" Maretta replied.

"The kids. Paul left several messages on my phone. Glen called him. They want to know why we aren't calling them back."

"I thought we agreed not to check our messages for a few days. Give them a chance to miss us," Maretta placed the water glass down firmly and stood up. She began to pace, looking for something that obviously wasn't there. "You didn't call him back, did you?"

"No," Joan replied, regret seeping into her. "I think we should go home. I've had enough adventure."

"Go home?" Maretta's mouth flew open as she turned swiftly and looked down at Joan. "We've just got started!"

Maretta began to gather her things. She opened the new designer luggage she picked out last night and transferred her things from the linen bag in a fury, like a squirrel stashing away its nuts.

Joan got up and headed for the bathroom. She brushed her teeth, splashed water on her face and leaned over to look at the woman in the mirror. She reached up and fluffed the matted side of her hair until it was almost as lovely as yesterday. Her shoulders softened and she leaned back. She turned her head to the left and admired the view, then to the right. *Even better,* she thought. *I should have colored my hair years ago. I feel ten years younger.* She struck a pose. *Well, maybe we can go one more day. She came up with a plan.*

"If you want to go, go," Maretta shouted through the door. "I'm continuing on."

Joan opened the door. She didn't like the tone of Maretta's voice. She knew damn well she could go if she wanted to, she didn't need her permission. Looking into her friend's indignant eyes she saw fear, pain, and sadness and her chest clenched. "Okay, okay, but let's not stay here."

"Agreed," Maretta said as she reached up and twirled the locket.

Maretta handed the valet a wad of bills.

He looked down at the stack of fifties as his eyes bulged from his head. "Thank you!"

Maretta praised him with gratitude. Sofia sat parked next to them in perfect condition.

Joan watched curiously as police and security ran into the front door. "What's going on?" she asked the bellman standing on the curb. He leaned over and whispered into her ear.

The commotion began to attract Maretta's attention too. "Come on Joan, get in, before a bomb goes off."

They fastened on their seat belts and Maretta hit the gas. Errrr, the sound of tires screeching on the pavement made the valet jump back. Maretta drove right out onto the street without looking. An oncoming minivan skidded to a stop, nearly missing her backend. Undaunted, Maretta hit the gas harder and kept going, leaving the frazzled driver behind waving his hand in the air.

"What the hell was going on there? Why all the police and security?" Maretta wondered aloud to Joan.

"The bellman said that a bunch of retirees were pounding the slot machines demanding their money back. He said they were getting unruly."

"Gee, I should have thought of that," Maretta said looking straight ahead with a sheepish grin.

"Cape May, here we come," Joan said drawing in the fresh air through her nose. Giddiness overtook her. She hadn't been to Cape May in years but remembered it fondly as a place her family visited when she was a child. It's where she had her first kiss, with a boy named Billy, under the stars, the ocean splashing around them, their feet sinking into the sand.

"That is awfully nice of your old co-worker to allow us to stay at her cottage." Maretta said.

Joan nodded her head in agreement as they turned onto the Garden State Parkway, Hermes scarves neatly protecting their hair, sun shining on their faces and possibilities down the road.

Chapter 11

The park was full of screaming preschoolers chasing each other and vying for loudest kid on the planet. Julie sat on a bench in deep conversation with another mom, holding the baby against her breast.

"Where are you?" Glen asked.

"The playground," Paul answered, holding the phone in the crook of his neck. "Look, my wife has our day packed with activities. I'm going to try and make a stop at my Mom's, see if she is there. I don't know why they aren't answering."

"I'm really worried," Glen said.

"I'm really annoyed. I mean what the f — ," he shoved the phone in his back pocket so he could save his toddler from falling off the ladder. "Like I don't have better things to do, then go and try to hunt down grown women."

Glen scratched his head. He looked over at his luggage sitting in the corner, that he never unpacked. "Let me know if you find out anything else. I appreciate it. I'm sorry I'm not there."

"Yeah," Paul answered distracted. "Hey, don't jump from there, it's too high."

Glen stood up.

"Listen, I've got to go," Paul told Glen, the frustration in his voice sending guilt waves through Glen's body.

* * *

The giant, forest-green, wooden sign with gold-engraved lettering made Maretta's mouth start to water. The Lobster House. She could almost taste the chunk of lobster meat, dripping with salty, drawn butter glide along her tongue. She imagined the distinctive chewy, delicate crunch of the meat releasing a briny taste of the ocean between her teeth. "The Lobster House, we need to eat there," Maretta said to Joan as if she were her own personal tour guide.

Joan was in her own world. The familiar site of the bridge led them into a place she felt was the closest thing to paradise. A flutter of excitement tickled the inside of her. Every muscle in her body let go of the concerns. She let her right arm rest on the door, right above where the rolled down window was tucked away. Maretta's chatter faded into the background. *So many fond memories here, I'm glad we came.*

The one-lane street led them past buildings, mom-and-pop shops, and businesses catering to the sea-boatyards, deep sea fishing tours and whale-dolphin watching. "Dolphins! I love dolphins! Let's do that too," Maretta added to her itinerary as her head swayed back and forth searching for more opportunities. "Why didn't you ever tell me about this town. It's so cute! Are we still in New Jersey?"

"Watch!" Joan shouted as if she had just been tazered. Her stomach twisted into a sailors knot. Her hands flew up to the dashboard to brace for impact.

Maretta instantly turned her attention back to the road and jammed on the brakes.

A woman pushing a baby stroller with one hand in the crosswalk, while pulling an obstinate toddler in the other, scowled at Maretta.

Maretta hunched below the steering wheel, gave the woman a gentle wave and whispered, "sorry."

The screeching of the tires drew the attention of a handful of teenage boys hanging out in front of the baby-pink-colored ice cream store. "Hey, it's the Cool Grannies!" one of them announced to the others.

"You mean the ones Alejandro posted?" another exclaimed.

Without asking, they gathered on the edge of the sidewalk and held their cell phones up towards the car. Joan and Maretta smiled reluctantly. Each of them acknowledging that all the camera attention was getting to be a bit much.

"What is wrong with people these days," Maretta shook her head, then gently pressed down on the gas pedal. "Look at them, they all have their heads buried in their phones."

Joan shrugged in agreement. Her draining phone battery started to weigh heavier on her mind. She knew enough to turn it off last night to preserve any precious life it may have left. The bar was lit yellow when she made the quick call to her friend from the nursing home to ask if they could use her cottage. *I'll have to find a way to check it again later.*

They weaved through the neighborhoods filled with charming, small, cozy houses with front porches and inviting walkways. The front doors nestled between hydrangea and rose bushes. Tall trees, with lush canopies, covered the street with shade. Joan fed Maretta directions from her memory of past visits to her former nurse colleagues home.

"She said the realtor would meet us here at ten," Joan said as they pulled up alongside a weathered, grey fence.

Maretta looked up and slapped her palms up to hold her cheeks. "We are right across the street from a real lighthouse."

Joan's eyes followed up the eggshell-white lighthouse. The top surrounded by a brick-red metal cage with a walkway all around it. "We can go up to the top of it when it's open." Joan pointed to the east. "We can watch the sunrise on the beach over there." Then she pointed to the west. "It's a short walk to the beach that way, where the sunsets."

The car door sounded its age as Joan pushed it open and unfurled herself to a standing position. She leaned over the fence, and pulled a pale, yellow rose up to meet her nose.

The toot of a horn accompanied by a charismatic, "Hello," made their heads turn. A woman in a white BMW convertible waved her hand in the sky. She pulled in behind Maretta, then jumped out of the car and rushed to shake

Maretta's hand. "I hope you haven't been waiting long. I'm Colleen, the realtor."

"No, not at all," Joan replied.

Colleen held the house key attached to a navy rope, with a gold anchor on the end, in her hand. She offered to help carry luggage, but was shooed away. Instead she escorted them through the gate. They followed her down the gravel pathway lined with robust, blue hydrangeas in various stages of bloom, to the front door of the two-story wood-shingled cottage. "You have to jiggle it a little," she said, then turned the key and opened the door.

Warm sunlight beamed through the lace curtains surrounding the living room, showcasing sections of wood floor lighter than others. Oak shelves framed the lower half of the walls below the windows, for three quarters of the room. Each shelf firmly packed with books.

Maretta felt like she hit the jackpot again, "a lighthouse across the street and tons of books to read."

The realtor pushed aside the delicate curtains and began cranking a series of windows open, "It's a bit stodgy at first. No one has been here for a few weeks."

"It's perfect," Maretta said as she wandered ahead into the dining room, the floor creaking with each step. There on the hutch she found a pile of tourist brochures and raised them one by one. "Look at this, they have this beautiful local farm that gives tours, all these restaurants, and here is information about the dolphin boat tours we passed on the way in." She dove into the pile, rummaging through all the possibilities.

Joan briefly closed her eyes as her hands pressed against her stomach. A wave of gratitude washed over her. When she opened her eyes again, Maretta was sorting the various brochures into piles. *Maybe she will get enough fill here, and then she'll be ready to go home. At least she seems enthralled enough to stay put for a little while. And it is nice to be back.*

"Please, let me show you around the rest of the home," the realtor suggested. Maretta put down the brochures and followed as they were shown the downstairs bedroom and bath, the kitchen adorned with seashells along the window sills, the upstairs bedrooms: one with bunk-beds the other a matching wooden, queen-sized bed and vanity, and a hall, full bath. They were given a list of several suggested local favorite eateries, shown where the garbage was to be put outside and how to operate the outdoor shower. "Is there anything else I can do for you?'

"No," Joan replied as they finished the tour. "You have been very helpful. We really appreciate you accommodating us on such short notice."

"How long will you be staying," Colleen asked never letting go of her smile.

Joan waited to see if Maretta would answer first. The unanswered phone messages gnawing on her soul. She needed to find a private moment to check her phone again.

"There is so much to do here, we may stay a while. If it's okay, of course, with Joan's friend."

Joan felt like Maretta had just handed her the keys to the car. *Perfect, I can use the excuse that Ginny said we have to go when I'm ready to leave.* "I will need to check with Ginny.

Let me walk you to your car." Joan placed her hand on the realtor's shoulder and gently pushed her towards the deck stairs.

"Have fun," the realtor waved back at Maretta. Maretta turned her attention to the lighthouse.

"You wouldn't happen to have a phone charger, would you?" Joan whispered in the realtor's ear when they reached the BMW.

"What type of phone? I may, people leave their chargers in my car quite often." She reached over to the glove box, opened it, and pulled out a pile of black wires attached to plugs.

Joan's palms moistened with sweat as she sorted through the chargers not recognizing any that look like they would fit into her phone. "When did life get so complicated?" she muttered.

"Blessing and a curse these things," the realtor said as she held up her phone smiling.

"I don't think any of these will work," Joan said as she handed the tangled web back to Colleen.

"I'm sorry, sweetie," Colleen stuffed them back in the glove compartment. "Let me know if you need anything else and when you want to leave. The house isn't rented for the next two weeks. I can come and pick up the key when you leave."

Joan tried to block the conversation from reaching Maretta with her body. "Okay, we'll let you know. We don't want to keep you," she said. She backed away and willed her to leave.

"Okay, by now." Colleen started the engine and put the car into gear. She left behind a trail of music from a Beach Boys song.

The lighthouse dominating the clear blue sky caught Joan's attention too. A lighthouse, maybe it's a sign — a place for those who are lost to find their way back home. A shift occurred inside. She felt a wave of peace come over her. When she looked back to the deck, she didn't see Maretta.

"One o'clock, yes, two please," Maretta held her phone to her ear with one hand while she rummaged through her purse and pulled out a credit card with the other. She read off the numbers, expiration date and code on the back. "Terrific, we're looking forward to it." She nodded at Joan, and jotted down directions on the back of an envelope she found. "We're all set to go on a dolphin watch this afternoon. Isn't this exciting?"

In an even tone Joan responded, "yes." Thinking more about it, however, it became clear that it might be a good idea. It was, after all, a perfect day for a boat ride; only a light wind, no clouds, they would probably only need a light sweater. "Yes," she repeated this time in a more upbeat tone, not letting on that she had her own plan.

Chapter 12

There was an eerie, abandoned feeling. Paul sensed it as soon as he pulled up to his mother's driveway. The garbage can was still on the side of the street next to the mailbox with its top flipped open even though pick up was two days ago. Finally, he could think more clearly. The kids slept in the back seat; their heads flopped to side. He tried to explain to Julie, but she was just annoyed that her plans were being interrupted. She sat rigid, looking out the window.

He pulled the car into the driveway and drove slowly up the slight incline. The front door was closed which was normal, but as he got closer to the garage doors he noticed the light above the backdoor was still on.

"I'll be right back," he said. He unbuckled his seatbelt, and got out of the car, leaving the engine running. He walked up to the garage doors and peered in the windows. No car. He looked around the yard. The birdfeeder was empty and the flowers in the patio pots were begging for a drink. He walked up the short flight of steps to the backdoor and peaked in through the small panes of glass in between the curtains. No signs of life. No mail lying on the counter, no dirty dishes in the sink, no basket of laundry waiting to be folded on a kitchen chair. Tidy, too tidy. He noticed a pad of paper on the table with a pen lying next to it.

He tapped on the door out of respect, not really expecting an answer, then reached into his pocket. "Shit, the keys are in the car."

"Something's not right," he told Julie as he reached in and turned the ignition off.

"You're going to wake the kids," Julie said in horror, then turned to look at the two. They didn't seem to notice. They gently snored in unison. She whispered, "what do you mean something isn't right?"

"My mom hasn't answered my calls in a couple of days. Aunt Maretta hasn't answered Glen's calls. The house looks empty. I'm going to check inside." He left the car door ajar, hoping not to awaken the dragons.

Inside, he lifted the pad and read the note written in Joan's handwriting. *Went for a ride with Aunt Maretta.* He let the pad fall and slap against his thigh. "Great."

"Everything okay?" Julie asked, leaning closer to Paul.

"We need to take a ride over to Aunt Maretta's," Paul answered and started up the car.

* * *

A shaggy-haired guy, wearing a faded, blue t-shirt with a white dolphin on the front and wrinkled khaki pants, leaned against the driftwood-colored piling at the end of the pier.

A two-story, steel ship painted white rocked gently behind him. The same dolphin image from the t-shirt was stenciled in blue along the side of the ship. Worn, white buoys, tied to the side of the boat, groaned as they were squeezed between the boat and the dock, over and over.

"Do you let senior citizens on first?" Maretta asked the young man. He unleashed the rope that prevented people from boarding. She reached over and held onto the nearest stable object as if she might otherwise fall.

"Are you handicapped?" he asked. He glanced at the crowd building behind her.

"I just had my hip replaced. I need to be extra careful." Maretta replied, placing her other hand on her hip. She added, "Doctor's orders."

"Okay, have a seat right here on this bench, and I will let you on first when it's time." He left them waiting so he could help the crew undo ropes.

Joan's fingers touched her parted lips. She let them expand so that her hand shielded her mouth as she whispered, almost inaudibly, "There is nothing wrong with your hip."

Maretta mimicked Joan's hand gesture as she replied, "Look at all these people. They are already pushing and shoving in line. If we don't get on the boat first, and get a seat, we just may get shoved, fall down and then we will have a broken hip."

Joan let her hand fall to her lap and turned away. She took another deep breath of the salty sea air and let the soaring seagulls distract her thoughts.

"I hope we don't get seasick," they overheard a nearby passenger say.

Maretta turned quickly to look at Joan.

"Do you think we'll get sick?" Maretta asked. "You're a nurse."

"I sure hope not, we just ate those bagels." Joan replied. "And being a nurse doesn't mean I am a walking medical encyclopedia or have a magical medical crystal ball."

The young man returned to the crowd and said to Maretta, "Okay, you can go first."

The crowd surged forward. Joan grabbed Maretta's arm firmly as they pushed their way to the front of the line. Maretta limped slowly. "Excuse me, careful, she just had surgery. I'm a nurse."

No one else was allowed to board until the two were firmly planted in the best seat on the ship on the upper deck. Maretta's chest thrust out with accomplishment. While they waited for the rest of the passengers to board, Joan got up and looked over the railing next to her seat. Below a school of fish swam along the top of the water in unison, like ballet dancers. Sailboats, fishing boats, private yachts chugged their way beside them, heading into and out of the harbor.

"Good afternoon, everyone," a chipper voice rang out over a loud speaker. "My name is Ray and I will be your host for today's trip. Todd will be our captain and my mates, Emma and Raj, are here to also make your dolphin watching experience a safe and fun one." Ray went through the safety procedures — life preservers, lifeboat and seasickness protocol followed by outlining where the comfort stations and snack bar locations were.

Joan returned to her seat. "I'm not so sure you will be able to get first dibs on the lifeboat if we get into trouble."

"Maybe I should have brought a cane to beat people back."

The boat's engine revved twice, the deck hands hustled, and before they knew it, they were headed out to sea.

"We'll be looking for dolphins today, we'll need everyone to be on the lookout. There are many different species of dolphins. The ones we hope to see today are bottlenose dolphins. The dolphins that swim off our shores here, in Cape May, spend summer here and usually winter down in the Carolinas."

In front of the two, three boys sat with their heads leaning deeply forward. A woman, wearing no make-up and a white, stained sweatshirt sat next to the trio on the end. Maretta peaked over one of the boy's shoulders and confirmed what she thought was happening. The mother turned and watched Maretta lean back into her seat.

"How many times do I have to tell you to put those phones away," the mother yelled.

Maretta could hear grumbling as she watched the boys scramble to put their phones in their pockets. As soon as the mother began talking to a Mom sitting across the aisle, the boys exchanged glances and pounced on the opportunity to resurrect their phones.

"I'm so glad we raised our boys before all this technology," Maretta said to Joan, who shook her head in agreement.

"Kids today don't even know how to have a conversation." Her eyes became glued to the boys' heads even though she wanted to be looking out at the open sea, hoping to spot dolphins. When the mother turned to see the boys on their phones again, she repeated her command even louder this time.

Making sure she said it loud enough for the mother to hear, Maretta said, "If those were my kids, I would rip those phones from their little hands and throw them overboard."

The mother looked back at Maretta. "If they weren't so expensive and a necessary evil in today's world, I just might do that."

The boys slid their phone back into their pockets and pouted.

"They play games, interact with friends — constantly. Schools are asking them to do homework, and search for information, on devices. With three boys, I need them to keep on top of their schedules — school, sports, music lessons, tutoring, religious studies. Some days I feel more like a taxi driver than a mom," she spoke out in the direction of the water.

Maretta noticed her chipped nail polish as she reached her hand up to run it through her youngest son's hair. Below her heavy eyes, dark bags lay and she looked as if she probably skipped washing her hair this morning, maybe even yesterday too. Maretta opened her mouth, and then closed it, not sure she should ask about the boys' father. She wanted to hand her some advice about how she parented her sons but something held her back. This woman looked too tired to take anything else in. *A good whooping* came across her thoughts. *No, it's not the kids' fault.* "Parenting is hard," was the best she could come up with. Even she wasn't convinced it was the right thing to say, but she felt like the woman had hit the ball in her court. She wanted to return the serve.

"We have a touch tank up here if anyone would like to come and see. Emma will be sharing some fun facts about these animals. Come on up."

"Why don't you guys go and see," the mother nudged. They all shook their heads no.

Feeling her blood pressure rise, Maretta stood up, crawled over Joan and held onto the steel railing. She looked out at the endless horizon. *The sea is full of infinite possibilities and wonder,* she thought. *Where are you dolphins?*

"We are going to hand out some binoculars so you can help us spot dolphins or whales. We have had an influx of whale sightings the past few years," the captain announced.

"How about looking for dolphins with binoculars?" the mother pleaded.

"No."

"This is boring," another added.

Maretta accepted a pair of binoculars and began scanning the wild waters like a pirate looking for treasure. When her arms tired she let them rest on the railing, holding the binoculars tight. After a few minutes she began panning back and forth, desperately hoping to see dorsal fins break through the waves.

"How long are we going to be out here?" the boy closest to Maretta whined.

Maretta tightened her core and stood up straight, with purpose. She held the binoculars more firmly to her eyes then fixed on a far-off point like an English setter who spots a duck, "Shark!"

Joan jolted out of her daydream and jumped out of her seat to look. She pressed her glasses tightly against her face, as if that might allow her to see farther.

"Shark!" Maretta sounded again, not moving her direction.

The boys jumped out of their seats and stood side by side, squeezed next to Maretta.

"Where?"

"I don't see it."

"Way out there, it's huge," Maretta said emphasizing huge and keeping a fierce lock on the spot. "Oh my God, he just jumped out of the water!"

The boys scurried to their mother, each begging for the pair of binoculars she held. She offered them to her sons; the tallest reached up and grabbed them from her hands.

"I can see his dorsal fin ripping through the waves, he's HUGE," Maretta said loudly.

The eldest boy threw the binoculars to his face. His brothers leaned in close to him.

"I want to see."

"Let me have them."

"Mom!!"

Maretta allowed herself to sneak a peek at the boys. She looked back through the binoculars and added, "He's coming this way."

Maretta pulled the binoculars away from her face and offered them to Joan with a wink, "Want to see?"

Joan grinned, and nodded enthusiastically, then held them up to her eyes. She gave it a few minutes, then said in a disappointed tone while her shoulders shook, "I don't see it."

Maretta reached her hand to guide the binoculars to the spot she was looking at, then said to Joan, making sure the boys could hear, "Look, right there, give it a minute because sometimes the waves hide his fin, it's huge."

"I want a turn!"

The two younger boys began greedily tried to grab the binoculars gripped fiercely by their brother.

"I haven't seen it yet, where is it?"

"You aren't looking hard enough, "Maretta reached over and angled his focus in the same direction as Joans.

"I see it," Joan shrieked. "You're right, it is HUGE."

"Where?" the eldest cried, desperately.

"Give them to me!" the other two screamed.

Maretta couldn't hold back the laughter as she watched them battle. She looked back at the mother who sat with a playful smile on her face. She gave Maretta the thumbs up sign.

The youngest boy caught the secret glance between the two. "You're lying, there's no shark."

The eldest let the binoculars fall from his face. His mouth opened in disbelief.

"What if there was a shark, or a dolphin, or a humongous whale out there? You boys would never know it with your faces buried in those phones," Maretta said flippantly. She mirrored the middle one putting her hands on her hips.

"Dolphins! Stern side about 100 feet out." Ray announced excitedly over the PA system.

"Which is the stern side?" Joan asked. She looked all around the ship to see where other people were looking. The wind started to blow stronger. Quickly, she surmised it was the back where the crowd grew.

Maretta handed the youngest her binoculars and watched him squeeze his way to the railing on the back of the boat, his brothers in hot pursuit behind him. The captain turned the ship so everyone could see the pod of dolphins swim along in the waves. The boys' mother looked on, a tear of joy dripped from her eye.

Chapter 13

Paul watched his wife sitting in the car, flicking her phone screen. He walked back to Maretta's back stairs and sat down.

"They aren't home and your Dad's Thunderbird is gone." Paul told Glen, and then told him about the note.

"Where would they go? Why wouldn't they answer their phones?" Glen asked concerned.

Julie ran up to Paul, "You're not going to believe this. Your Mom and Maretta, they are all over social media," she held her phone out. "My friend, Sara, just texted to tell me. Her son recognized your mom in this picture."

"Hold on," Paul said and put his phone down on the step. He reached over and took Julie's phone, studying it like he was trying to make a diagnosis from an x-ray. "What the hell did they do to their hair?"

Julie grabbed her phone and scrambled to find more posts. "They were on the Jersey Turnpike. The more recent posts look like they are in some small town."

"Dude, I don't know what the hell is going on here," Paul

filled Glen in on the latest.

"I'm going to get a flight out there as soon as possible, keep me posted will ya?" Glen said.

"Yeah, of course," Paul confirmed.

Glen rang his brother.

"Hello?" Andy said with sleep still in his voice.

"Get up," Glen said anxiously as he looked down at his watch in disgust. "Mom and Aunt Joan are acting crazy."

Andy rolled over and listened. "Good for them."

"They're driving Sofia," Glen emphasized the car's name still trying to accept that his mother would risk damaging her.

"You're just concerned about the car. Grass hasn't even grown over Dad's grave and you already have your claws out." Sophia was always a bone of contention between the two brothers. The family joke was that Glen was Charlie's son and Andy was his mother's son, but Andy never really found it funny. Charlie invested a lot of time grooming Glen to grow up and use his head to work, not his hands. He tried to do the same with Andy early on, but Andy was different. Not a numbers guy, he was creative, artsy. Charlie didn't know what to do with that. Charlie was so proud when Glen got the big finance position out in California.

"That's ridiculous," Glen rebutted. "I don't know why I am wasting time talking to you, I'm going to catch a plane and find them."

* * *

"Where to next?" Maretta looked over to Joan applying lipstick.

Before Joan could answer, three tween girls rushed over to them, their braces gleaming between wide grins. They stopped and bumped shoulders against each other as one blurted out, "Umm, are you the cool grannies? Our friends snapped a picture of you two, and your car, this morning and shared it."

Joan raised her sunglasses from eyes and looked at Maretta as her heart went from a walk to a trot pace. "Cool grannies?"

Maretta looked at the girls and nodded slowly at first, then began bobbing her head up and down with confidence. "Why yes, yes, we are. Would you like a picture?"

"Yeah," the girls sang in unison, their grins growing wider.

Maretta leaned closer to Joan and smiled. Joan put her sunglasses back, her pulse stepped up to a gallop. She smiled unconvinced this was a good thing to be doing, but eager to get out of this situation. The girls snapped away with their phones.

"Cool, thanks so much," the one with wire-rimmed glasses said.

"Abbie is going to be so jealous that we found them," another giggled while she plucked away at her phone.

"Okay, bye girls," Joan said. She nudged Maretta to get going.

"Thank you!" The girls repeated and walked away, side by side, with a spring in their step.

"How do these kids not trip or run into things?" Joan remarked.

Maretta shrugged, "or get run over."

When they reached the end of the marina driveway Maretta stopped. "Left or right?"

"Left," said Joan. "Let's go down to the boardwalk. I could use a long walk, shake off these sea legs."

Maretta turned left and crawled along the route Joan directed her to take. With each turn she grew to love this quaint town even more. Cute little shopping sections, lined with cobbled-stone walkways through the center. Flowers were everywhere; dripping from baskets attached to street-lights, tucked neatly into window boxes and flowing from pots along stairs. The community was like one giant bouquet. Evidence of the care, and attention to the simple details, that made life worth living, was everywhere they turned. Families meandered together. Couples sat sipping coffee at outdoor tables looking adoringly into each other's eyes while touching fingertips. Pups walked along side their owners panting gently, looking like they, too, were glad to be on vacation.

The dress was casual, but somewhat preppy. Men wore khaki shorts, button- down, cotton shirts left untucked, in an array of pastel colors. Many of the women wore flowery, loose-fitting dresses and flat or low-heeled shoes. The kids' uniform was simple t-shirts and shorts, sneakers without socks. The crowds moved in harmony. The pace was slow. The mood was contagious. Unaware, Maretta's breathing slowed, her hands sank to the lower part of the steering wheel and her grip loosened.

"Up ahead is the Victorian house section," Joan said pointing down the road ahead of them. "You're going to love this."

Joan was right; Maretta was in awe of the historic homes. Slowly, they drove passed each home ornately detailed to look like a two or three-story life-sized gingerbread house. Gables, turrets and hand-carved, custom- patterned porch fences adorned each home in unique colors rarely used on a house — purple with green trim, brown with orange trim, pink with yellow trim.

"We are going to need to come back and walk around these neighborhoods. It is just too much to try and take in while driving."

"There are more than six hundred Victorian era buildings, the whole town is a designated National Historic Landmark," Joan explained, her tone proud. With each block, a part of her younger self came alive. So many memories of summers spent here.

The midday, blaring sun made itself known as they reached Beach Avenue where the two-mile-long boardwalk ran parallel it. Sandy beach and the big blue ocean ran along on the other side of it.

"There's a spot over there," Joan pointed and Maretta jumped at the opportunity to snatch it noticing there weren't any others in sight.

Before they could gather their purses and slide out of the car, they were again, swarmed by teenagers. Convinced it was easier to just appease their requests, the two smiled, posed, and answered questions.

A couple around the same age as Maretta and Joan

stopped on the boardwalk and peered down at the crowd.

"Are they famous?" the gentleman asked the closest teen.

The teen turned and looked up, shielding his eyes from the sun. "They are the cool grannies. They are all over social media."

As the teen turned away, the gentleman shrugged, looked at his wife, who shrugged back at him. He pulled out his phone and snapped a picture. "I'll put it on our Facebook page."

The teen turned back overhearing him. "Be sure you add the #coolgrannies hashtag," he said holding his two hands up, letting both pointer and index fingers cross each other into a numbers sign.

"What's a hashtag?" the gentlemen asked perplexed.

"The number sign. Put it before coolgrannies, all one word, on your post. That way other people who are following them can find it. That's how we found out about them. Everyone in Cape May is looking for them," the teen said.

"Not everyone," the older woman stated. "We were just going for a walk, enjoying ourselves. Who knew we would be getting involved in a grannie hunt?"

Joan squeezed herself out of the car, went around to Maretta's side and pulled her out of the car and through the crowd, "Sorry, we need to get going," she told the onlookers. She thrust her head down and plowed ahead, Maretta in tow. She turned and ordered Maretta to walk faster.

Dutifully, Maretta picked up her pace and once they were free from the crowd shouted at Joan, "this is getting ridiculous."

The two climbed the half-dozen, cement steps up to the boardwalk level. Maretta didn't even look back to see if the car would be okay. She pulled her arms up, clenched her fists, and moved them back and forth along her sides in an attempt to propel herself further ahead. Joan was already a good two car lengths ahead of her.

It wasn't long before the baking heat and the vigorous cardiac exercise left them gasping for air. Joan stopped and let Maretta catch up. She looked behind; they were far enough away now. *Maybe, without the car, we can wander around in peace.*

Half bent over, Maretta let her hands rest on her knees. She raised her head and said, "Maybe we should sit for a minute."

Joan agreed and they sat down on one of the many park benches. Each bench was the same; they all faced the sea, and lined the boardwalk for as far as the eye could see. They all faced the same direction, towards the sea. Maretta let out a huff and leaned over resting her arms on her thighs. Her head fell like a rag doll.

"Are you okay?" Joan's breath was nearly back to normal.

"Yeah, just not used to running from the paparazzi," she joked.

"Was it always like this when you went for a ride with Charlie?" Joan threw her arm up to rest on the back of the bench. She readjusted her glasses with her other hand.

"Sofia always turned heads," Maretta replied. She sat up straight and wiped her forehead with the back of her hand. "But, this picture taking is new. We were never mobbed like this."

Joan chuckled, "I wonder what Charlie would have made of all of this?"

"I'm not exactly sure. To be honest, he wasn't one who particularly liked to be the center of the attention. But, I can tell you, he is probably up there having a good, hearty laugh watching us." Maretta leaned back, let her arms drape by her side and closed her eyes.

Joan noticed her friend looked a little pale. A sudden flash of light made her eyes squint. She leaned closer to the glimmering metal plate attached to the back of the bench they sat upon. "In gratitude for the family weekends spent with Grandma Lily." she read aloud.

Maretta opened her eyes, looked at Joan, and then followed Joan's gaze to the memorial plaque.

Joan checked the bench next to them. It had a plaque, as well, on the back of the bench. Curious, she walked over and read it aloud to Maretta. "In memory of Roger and Ethel Tyler-loving parents, grandparents and faithful friends." Together they went on to the next bench and the next, taking turns reading the engraved tributes. Each one inscribed with sentiments of family, good times had at Cape May and/or loved ones fondly remembered.

"I'll be lucky if my sons engrave my tombstone," Maretta said.

Joan said nothing at first. The somber reality of the loneliness her friend would be left with, now that Charlie was gone. Sure, she had Joan and friends back home, but it wasn't the same as family.

"Would you consider moving closer to one of your

sons?" Joan asked gingerly.

"Hell, no," Maretta replied. "For what? They have no family of their own. They are always working. I'd be stuck in a new place where I wouldn't know anyone."

Joan sighed, relieved by Maretta's answer. Her life wasn't exactly a Norman Rockwell picture either. They needed each other.

"Don't feel bad," Joan said adding a splash of sarcasm to the situation. "I told my son I want to be cremated, maybe have him spread my ashes out in a beautiful ocean like this one." She started walking and Maretta followed. As they let their thoughts drift out to sea, Joan added, "But, knowing Paul, he will probably get overwhelmed and stuff me on a closet shelf somewhere. Then his wife will get in a mood someday, take my urn out to the compost pile and dump me there."

Although Maretta didn't really believe Joan's family would be so heartless, she patted her on the shoulder and said, "Well, let's make a deal. If I go first, you take care of me, if you go first, I'll take care of you."

"And what if we die at the same time?"

Without skipping a beat, "Hopefully, we won't give a shit and we'll be off having a good time together."

Joan laughed, "Deal."

Maretta pulled her pink linen shirt down around her hips and wiped away imaginary wrinkles from the sleeves. She scanned the shops across the street. Their conversation was making her feel edgy, leaving her with a weird, uncomfortable energy charging through her body. "Look, across the street, fresh lobster rolls. You hungry?"

"For lobster rolls, sure," Joan agreed. "I thought you wanted to go to The Lobster House?"

"You can never eat too much lobster, we'll go there for dinner one night while we are here."

As they crossed the street, Joan suddenly lost her appetite. Guilt settled in like an uninvited guest who decides to stay for dinner on the night you planned on having cereal for supper. She knew she would need to tell Maretta soon.

The humongous light swirled around and around, like a child on a carnival ride, as soon as the sun tucked itself to sleep. The rhythm of sea seemed to soften. Those who had ventured to the beach, to ceremoniously witness the end of a day, began to gather their belongings and trudge home across the sand.

Maretta and Joan lingered, letting their toes explore under the warm sand. They said nothing; the long day of adventures left their brains on pause. If it weren't for a sudden gust of cool air that made Joan shiver, they may have fallen asleep right there on the beach.

"I think it's time to go in," Joan decided.

Maretta agreed, stood and wiped the sand off her backside as best she could. With sandals in hand, she stopped to watch the rotating light atop the pillar of strength. "Charlie used to say a lighthouse is a sailors best friend."

Joan felt a chill run up her spine and the hairs on her arms stood up. *I wonder if that is Charlie showing us the way.*

Chapter 14

The lace curtains waved like flags in the wind. Fresh morning air ushered into the room. The breeze seemed to clear Joan's thoughts that had been playing ping-pong in her head since she awoke.

Call my son now, before Maretta decides to move on to a new place.

No, don't call. Maretta will kill me; she'll feel so betrayed.

Joan sat like a statue on the edge of the bed, careful not to let it make any creaking noise and wake her sleeping friend upstairs. She gnawed softly on one of her knuckles until she finally mustered the courage to turn her cell phone on. *This is ridiculous, my hair is going to turn grey again just from worrying.* She watched the screen light up and went go through its rebooting process. She prayed with all her might that it would have enough battery power left.

Battery low.

First, she listened to the messages, each one more urgent than the next. Then the bomb, "Mom, what the hell is going on? We see you and Maretta on social media driving Uncle Charlie's car. Call me!"

She had heard enough.

She scrolled through the contacts and pressed on Paul's number. "Hurry, hurry," she whispered as her eyes wandered around the room and settled on the ceiling.

"Hello?" answered her daughter-in-law, Julie. Joan could hear her grandson babbling something about cereal in the background.

"Julie, it's me, Joan. Can I talk with Paul?" she whispered, "quick."

"Joan," Julie's tone a blend of surprise, relief and aggravation. "Where are you? You have us all worried."

"Look, my phone battery may run out any second. I really need to speak with Paul."

"He just ran out to get some milk, we ran out. He left his phone behind. I'm so glad I answered it. Are you okay?"

"I'm fine," Joan stood up and started pacing around the room. "Listen, grab a pencil and paper. I don't have much time."

Julie began to feel nervous. She obeyed the command, opened the kitchen junk draw, and dug through it until she found a pen and an old receipt to write on. She scribbled on it to wake up the ink. "Okay, what do you want me to write?"

Joan dictated the address where they were staying. "Tell him to come and get me today."

"Cape May? Isn't that all the way near the bottom of New Jersey? It will take him a few hours to get there."

Silence interrupted their conversation. Simultaneously, although separated by miles, they pulled their phones away from their ears, held them at arms length and looked at the screens.

Julie's screen said call ended.

Joan's screen was completely black. "I hope she got all that," Joan said to herself. She tucked the phone into her purse and began wringing her hands. The floor above her began creaking like an old wooden ship. *All I can do now is wait.* She looked at her watch. *I just need to keep us here until the early afternoon.*

Just until this afternoon, she repeated to herself. She opened the bedroom door and headed to the kitchen where she could hear Maretta fumbling with the coffee maker.

"Good Morning," Joan sang. "Oh, let me help you with that," she added, gently trying to nudge Maretta away from the coffee machine.

"I've got this," Maretta growled. "You're awfully cheery this morning."

"Just had a perfect nights sleep, that's all," Joan reached into the cabinet and pulled out the can of coffee. Her hands were shaking, she babbled on about nothing important. She pulled the top off with too much might, coffee grinds sprayed across the room. "Oh my, oh my," she repeated, then grabbed a paper towel and dove for the floor to wipe them up.

"I think that was the last of the coffee," Maretta said. She exhaled a breath of frustration. "You know how I am if I don't get my morning coffee." She held both hands up in the air, all fingers bent and facing forward like claws. Her entire face clenched and she showed her teeth.

"Maybe there is some tea," Joan attempted.

"That won't do it," Maretta yanked a paper towel from the roll and began gathering the grinds that fell onto the countertop like a bulldozer moving soil.

"I can take a run to the store," Joan countered. She tried to stand from her kneeling position, fumbled, and let go off all the coffee she had just gathered in her towel.

"This is ridiculous," Maretta said as she went to the kitchen closet. "There must be a broom in there."

Joan beat her to the closet and checked Maretta out of the way like a hockey player.

"Ow," Maretta slapped Joan on the arm reactively, then stood back, her lips pressed together while her legs widened their stance and her arms crossed. She watched her friend, normally the calm in the storm, buzz around the kitchen like a tornado, talking non-stop as she swept and re-swept the coffee grinds.

"Maybe it's a blessing in disguise," Maretta interrupted Joan's non-sense chatter. "There is a pancake place down the road. I haven't had pancakes in years. Ever since I saw that place when we drove in, I've been craving blueberry pancakes. I hope they make them with the blueberries in the pancake, not that blob of jelly stuff on top."

"Pancakes?" Joan squeaked.

"Yes, pancakes. You know flapjacks? Those flat bread like

things you drown in butter and syrup?" Maretta teased, still holding her folded arm stance.

"I know what pancakes are," Joan snapped back. She swept a pile of coffee grinds into the dustpan. She paused there and thought. *Breakfast, not a bad idea, might kill some time.* "Good idea. Let's get dressed and go for pancakes."

The hostess dressed in a navy blue, short-sleeved-collared shirt and white shorts pulled two laminated menus from her podium and said, "Follow me." She led Maretta and Joan through two separate dining rooms before stopping at the entrance of a bright, sunny, window-filled room resembling a conservatory. "Pick any table you like."

Before Maretta could pull a chair out from the two top nearest her, the only other customer in the room, said, "Anyone except that one." He lifted his coffee cup up to his mouth, took a sip, and then held it between his hands. "That one is George's."

Maretta scowled at the man whose few remaining grey hairs on his head matched his neatly trimmed beard. Unfazed, he took another sip of coffee.

"Come on," Joan urged and went to sit at the table in the far corner. The last thing she wanted was for Maretta to decide to go somewhere else.

The hostess scrunched her shoulders towards her head. "Sorry, I forgot, that is George's usual seat. I'm surprised he isn't here by now, he's a steady regular."

"That's okay, honey, we are fine right here," Joan comforted her, opened the menu and perused the choices.

"Your waitress, Sandy, will be right with you."

Maretta's eyes made a beeline to the pancake offerings. "Good, they have blueberry," and she put the menu down.

"Good morning, I'm Sandy. Coffee?"

"Yes, please," Joan answered.

Maretta nodded and held her cup up. "Do you put the blueberries in the pancakes or put that blueberry glop on the top?" Maretta asked.

"In the pancakes," the waitress said, "Eww, I hate when it is that glop."

Maretta smiled, feeling she made an instant friend. "I'll have the pancakes then."

"I'll have the same," Joan said, handing her menu over.

"Well, look what the cat just dragged in," the man on the other side of the room said. A casually dressed man, comparable in age to those already in the room, waddled in and took the seat Maretta originally wanted. "Where've you been, George?"

"Had to put gas in my car, forgot about the lines now that tourist season is starting," George sat, opened the paper napkin and mushed it into his lap. He looked over at the ladies and smiled, holding his gaze uncomfortably long.

Maretta and Joan instantly looked into their coffee cups.

"You ladies own that beauty outside?" he asked, quite sure of himself that it was they who owned that car, since he knew all the cars the regulars owned.

Joan and Maretta looked at each other, waiting for the other to answer him. Joan kicked Maretta under the table. Maretta said nothing, not wanting to engage George who she already sized up to be a character.

Joan shifted in her seat as if it was a hot plate. "It's hers."

"1963? It's a beauty," he repeated. "I'll have my usual, Sandy, and maple syrup for my coffee, please."

"Heart attack special?" The other man said shaking his head. "George, I don't know how you defy the odds."

"God doesn't want me ruining heaven," George chuckled at his own joke, and then proceeded to pour maple syrup into his coffee. "You know what they say, only the good die young."

The room became quiet. Joan's eyes explored her surroundings. There were pictures of locals and celebrities on one wall, two large beach paintings on another and glass art hung on the windows. A commercial for car insurance played on the radio. Maretta folded the edges of her placement like origami. The smell of bacon intensified.

Sandy delivered a large oval plate stacked with biscuits covered in a creamy, sausage gravy, eggs sunbathing in the center, and strips of bacon leaning off the side. "Need anything else, George?"

"No, honey, that should do it," He leaned closer to the plate and stabbed a biscuit, loaded it with extra gravy and introduced it into his mouth open as wide as a baby bird waiting for its mother to feed it. He purred with delight, his jaw rotated, "Mmmmm."

Joan and Maretta's pancakes, loaded with blueberries, were delivered next. All conversation took a backseat to the meals, each of the diners satisfying their pallets, while the warm morning sun streamed through the windows. Songs from the local radio station serenaded them until the disc jockey interrupted to bring them the local weather.

"We are starting off with great weather this morning here in Cape May — sunny, going to a high of seventy-five. This afternoon we will probably see some thunderstorms come through. The wind is from the south at about ten miles per hour."

Sandy made the rounds refilling coffee cups. The four continued to shovel their meals into their mouths, occasionally dabbing their lips with their napkins.

The radio disc jockey provided the only chatter. "Hey folks, how many of you remember this oldie but goody? 'Do you think I'm sexy?' by Rod Stewart."

The smash hit song from 1979 ignited the room with new energy. Sandy began to shake her hips as she held the coffee pot steady in her right hand. "I love this song," she said, and then left the room. The next thing they knew the volume was turned up.

The man on the far side of the room began tapping his foot to the beat. Joan let her hand rest on the table, her fork rested on the edge of the plate. Her eyes drifted to the outdoors in a dreamy state.

Maretta leaned closer to her pancakes, shoveling them in faster. Her stomach began to quiver. Feeling as if she was being watched, she slowly turned her head to face George. He looked away.

George began performing a chair-dancing version of John Travolta's Saturday Night Live finale, while chomping like a cow chewing cud.

Maretta chewed faster.

Joan began to sway as if she were a palm tree on a Caribbean beach enjoying the ocean breeze.

"Such good memories of this song. My husband used to dance around the kitchen like he was one, hot tamale. I would pretend I was embarrassed and he would insist that I dance with him, never taking no for an answer." She was grinning like a schoolgirl in her own world.

Maretta tapped her fork on her plate in an attempt to get Joan's attention. "Don't egg him on", she whispered anxiously.

Joan sat unfazed. She took a leisurely sip of her coffee.

"This was my theme song back in the good old days. Got the girls every time with this one," George announced. He stood up and lifted his hands in the air and gyrated his hips. His gut jiggled. He shimmied over to the ladies table.

Maretta shielded her face with her hand. Joan turned to look at George and batted her eyelashes. Her cheeks felt a surge of heat.

"Want to dance?" he asked, holding his hand out to Joan never pausing his hip motion.

Before Maretta could answer, Joan said, "Sure." She removed her napkin from her lap, placed it on the table, stood and placed her left hand in Georges. Maretta sat with her mouth gaping. Her head turned and her eyes met the guy's sitting across the room. He raised his eyebrows; Maretta buried her face back into her plate, wishing there was somewhere to hide. *Oh, good Lord.*

Maretta couldn't resist. She had to sneak a peek at Joan.

Joan merged closer with George, then stepped back and shimmied. Maretta sat up straighter, put her fork down. Her chest began to warm. *When was the last time I saw Joan looking this happy?* She wondered. The restaurant transformed into a dance floor of geriatric diners morphed into young adults.

"Yup, that is a goodie," the DJ concluded, as the music faded away. "Hope that got you feeling spicy! Speaking of spicy, have any of you seen those old ladies driving around in that white classic Ford Thunderbird? They have become something of a sensation here in Cape May. If you see them, take a picture and be sure to tag us in your social media posts."

The station broke to a commercial.

"Is he talking about you ladies?" George asked. He let go of Joan's hand.

Joan bowed her head, then looked up at him. "Yes, they seem to like calling us Cool Grannies."

"I didn't realize I was amongst the famous," he pulled his head back and released Joan's hand.

Joan blushed. She stood in place, not knowing what to say.

George reached over, took Joan's hand again and kissed the back of it tenderly. "Thank you for the dance." He walked her to the table, pulled her chair out, Joan floated into the chair. "How about I take you ladies to dinner tonight?"

Joan's smile ran away. Her body clenched.

Maretta caught Joan's smile and planted it on her own face. She gleefully said, "Oh, that would be very nice, but I have plans. Joan is available though."

Joan shot Maretta the evil eye.

Maretta smiled wider.

"It's a date, then. How about I pick you up at six?"

Joan faked a smile as her heel began to tap in rhythm with her rapid heartbeat.

"We are staying in the grey cottage right across the street from the lighthouse," Maretta told him.

"I know just where that is," George said as he left them, went to his table, pulled out a wad of bills and left them on his table. "See you at six."

The hissing sound of wind trying to creep in through the tiny crack where the convertible's roof met the frame of the car fought with the rising tension. It was the first time they rode with the top up. A musty smell replaced the crisp clean air. Joan sat with her arms folded across the chest and looked out the passenger window. Wide tree trunks whipped by one by one.

"I don't know why you are so mad, I was just trying to help," Maretta broke the silence.

Joan said nothing; she continued to look out the window as if she were studying something but not actually seeing anything, her thoughts claiming all her attention. *What a disaster. George is going to show up and no one will be there. I don't know how to get in touch with him. Paul should be at the house soon. Should I just let Maretta be surprised or should I tell her? How am I going to keep her at the house if she decides she wants to go out again? How did I get myself into this situation?* Joan began to chew on her bottom lip.

"Paul is coming for us," Joan announced and braced herself.

Maretta stomped on the brake, then let it up realizing there were cars right behind her. "What? What do you mean he is coming for us?"

"I called him this morning, gave him the address to the cottage and told him to come and get us," Joan nodded her head once in Maretta's direction very matter of fact. "They know we left town, took the car and they saw us in those pictures people keep taking. I don't understand, are we on the news or something?

"What do you mean us?"

"Maretta, we've got to go home. I know it's hard to lose a husband but you can't run away from the pain," Joan let her arms release and placed her hands together in her lap.

"I'm not running away," Maretta gave Joan a stern look then returned her eyes to the road as she gripped the steering wheel tighter. "I'm living my life. I'm not dead yet. I thought you were excited about this adventure too."

Joan listened but said nothing, knowing full well her friend would not react well to pity.

They pulled up to the cottage. Maretta jammed the car into park and jumped out of the car. "You can go home if you want, but I'm not." She slammed the door behind her and marched into the house.

The solid lighthouse stood undaunted by what occurred. The baby blue, cloudless sky above it soothed Joan as she stared at it, contemplating her next move. *If only you could talk. How many storms have you seen and yet you remain unmoved, firm, strong.* Joan gained strength from the motionless building. *It's time I do what I need to do.*

Chapter 15

Dark clouds loomed above the airplanes lined up on the tarmac. Glen finished off his third cup of coffee, crushed the cup in his hand and pitched it into the trash. He watched the clouds morph into deeper shades of grey to the right.

"Where are you?" Glen asked Paul, without any pleasantries.

"I'm halfway down the Garden State Parkway. I should be there in about two hours."

"I hope I don't get stuck here in Chicago, looks like a storm is coming in," Glen said. "I'm going to fly into Newark, rent a car and head down there."

"Good," Paul said feeling relieved. "You know how your Mom can be."

Paul dragged his foot along the carpet. "Yeah, you don't have to tell me. I will call you as soon as I land."

* * *

The sound of footsteps stomping back and forth above didn't surprise Joan. She went into her room and began to pack her things. A door slammed above followed by stairs creaking and the sound of luggage clobbering each step. Maretta stood in the bedroom doorway, her purse slung over her left shoulder, pulling her luggage with her right arm. She avoided looking directly at Joan, "Go home if you want. I'm continuing on!" She spun on her heels and left without waiting for an answer.

Joan stood, letting the silence settle. By the time she reached the living room window, Maretta was already pulling away. Joan looked up and begged the heavens to watch out for Maretta. There was nothing she could do now but wait.

Sophia escorted Maretta aimlessly around the neighborhoods allowing her to calm down. *I need to get out of this town,* Maretta concluded. She pulled into a gas station and handed the attendant a credit card. "Filler er up."

She turned to the attendant holding the gas nozzle. "How do I get out of this town?"

"Where do you want to go?" he replied.

Why is everyone making everything so damn complicated? "South," she barked.

"Well," he paused, replaced the hose into the pump, and waited for the receipt to spit out. "You can either drive back west and get on 95 or you can take the ferry over to Lewes and drive down along the coast. If you're not in a hurry, the coast would be much more scenic."

Maretta weighed her options. Avoiding the interstate sounded less stressful. "How do I get to the ferry?"

"It's not far," he said as he handed her the credit card and receipt, then gave her directions.

Maretta's heart began to pound like a bass drum when she turned into the road leading to the ferry terminal. She imagined a small port, with something like a tugboat, which would carry her, and maybe a few other cars, across the channel. Instead, she found large, automated gates and a massive modern building. Docked was an enormous multi-level ship that she would have assumed was a luxury cruise boat. She wiped her sweaty hands on her thighs one by one as she drove slowly towards the terminal building.

The freshly polished terminal floor gave off a lemony scent. It was nearly empty. The deep, drawn out, blast of a horn startled Maretta. She felt vibrations throughout her whole body. It stopped and then repeated. She rushed back out the double glass doors and watched the ship pull away from the dock. Deflated she went back in and stood with her head down.

"You just missed that one," a voice from behind a glass window empathized. "There is another one in a few hours, though."

Maretta walked over to the window, and peered at the old man with a sweet face. She scowled at him, "A few hours?"

"Yes, Ma'am," we have a little café where you can wait or there is a nice place to eat right along the beach just around the corner. He pointed behind her.

Maretta weighed her options. She was too tired to try and figure out how to get to the interstate. A leisurely boat ride definitely seemed the way to go. "I'll take a ticket for the next boat. How do I get to that beach?"

The ocean seems to cradle Cape May in her arms from all sides, Maretta thought as she made a right turn onto Beach Drive. Her shoulders hunched and her eyes squinted. She looked for the restaurant that the man at the ferry terminal recommended, Cape May Seaside Place. She stole a glance out at the angry, denim-blue sea thrusting waves on to the shore. The sight of dolphins cruising along the waves made her stop. "Sure, you're right there. I could have watched you right from the beach."

Relieved to find her destination, she pulled around back into the gravel parking lot, grateful to be able to hide the car. It only took a few miles for the painful reality to hit; it was a lot harder to drive without a co-pilot. The weight of the thought made her head fall onto her hands that rested on the top of the steering wheel.

The sound of another car creeping into the parking lot jolted her awake. *I better go inside before they want to take a picture.* She grabbed her purse and scurried around to the front entrance. The sun disappeared behind dark clouds.

Inside, a room filled with picnic tables, covered in blue-and-white-checked tablecloths, stood empty. In front of her, equally empty, a wood-laminated bar that offered seating on all sides. Wood-planked walls, painted white, were dotted with sea paraphernalia — beer lights and whimsical quotes like "Sunsets Are Free". Above the bar hung lime-green-painted oars, threaded with plastic beer pitchers ready to be filled. A life-sized, hand-carved sea captain who stood next to a brass ship wheel was the only soul in the place.

Maretta paused imagining that this place must fill up with casual, carefree patrons out for a good time. She took a whiff and to her surprise it smelled freshly mopped, not like beer left over from last night. A burly man with a short scruffy beard burst through the kitchen doors carrying a rack full of glasses.

"Are you open?" Maretta asked.

"We sure are," he said enthusiastically. "It's five o'clock somewhere, right?"

Still full from the pancakes, Maretta shimmied her way up onto a bar seat, disregarding the five o'clock comment, that seemed popular here, "whatever."

"What can I get you?" the bartender asked. He wiped his hands on a clean cotton towel.

Maretta looked up and down the bar. "A Budweiser." She paused and looked at the empty barstool beside her. "Make that two. In a can."

The bartender reached slowly into the refrigerator below the bar and pulled out two cans of Bud. He popped open the first one and placed it in front of Maretta.

She slid it along the bar until it sat in front of the empty stool next to her. "I'll have mine in a glass."

Confused, he reached up for a glass, tilted it sideways and let the cold, golden fluid pour into the glass. He let the foam settle for a moment before filling it to the rim. Then passed it to Maretta.

"I know this is your favorite," Maretta told the air to her right when the bartender returned to his duties. "Cheers." She lifted her glass towards the can, and then took a long sip.

The bartender wiped down the other side of the bar.

An eerie silence filled the room. Beads of water gathered around Maretta's glass. The can of beer sat untouched. The bartender stole a glance now and then at his only customer so far. The lunch crowd wouldn't start coming for another hour. He slid his way closer and strained to her what she was saying.

"Can you believe she left me?" Maretta said looking to her right. "She left me, just like you did." She turned back and looked at her drink, raised it and took another sip. Then another.

Chapter 16

Glen powered on his phone as soon as the plane hit the runway. There were messages waiting.

"Welcome to Newark," the flight attendant said, then continued with the usual instructions.

"Dude, your mother took off. I got my mom," Paul's message began. "We have no idea where she went. Julie is monitoring social media to see if anyone posts something, but so far no luck. I don't know what to do."

The exhaustion in his friend's voice made Glen angry.

Glen rang his brother, "She's gone, took off on her own, now what do we do?"

"What do you mean gone?" Andy asked.

Paul filled him in. "Do you think she is starting to lose it?"

"Listen, I hear your concern, but I don't think Mom is demented?" Andy answered.

"Well, I'm calling the police," Paul said, then hung up on his brother.

* * *

An ear-shattering shriek emitted from the bartenders pocket. He pulled his phone out and looked at the message on the screen curiously. He looked up at Maretta, she took another sip of beer, and then he looked back at his phone. "I'll be right back," he said as he bolted into the kitchen.

"Damn cell phones," Maretta grunted. She chugged the last of the beer and sat impatiently waiting for a refill. "You know, Sofia drives pretty well for an old gal," Maretta continued. "To be honest, I'm kind of surprised she got this far."

The bartender returned to find Maretta rambling on about the car — the poor mileage they were getting, how hard she was to park and all the unwanted attention she drew. "I'll have another," she told the bartender, she looked over at the can, "he'll have one too."

A clean-shaven man with curly, black hair strolled into the bar. "Hey, Tom. "He took a seat across from Maretta's. He watched Tom finish pouring Maretta's beer, then opened another can, placing it next to the other full ones.

"Guiness?" Tom asked the man, sitting with a perplexed look on his face. They both watched Maretta chatting away, pausing for a sip, and then babbling on to no one. Tom shrugged.

"Whatever," the guy said. "We've all got our isms. Ya, I'll have a Guiness."

* * *

"We just got a call," the policeman reported to Glen on his phone. "She's at Cape May Seaside Place. It's on Beach Drive."

"Thanks," Glen replied. "I'll take it from here." He Googled the location, pulled up the map on the phone then hit the directions button. It only took him ten minutes to get there. He pulled into the parking lot. The sight of Sophia sitting quietly in the shade of a giant oak tree, made him feel at ease.

Maretta was sitting with her back to Glen when he entered the bar. The bartender met Glen's eyes as soon as he noticed Glen paused at the door, watching Maretta. Tom placed a fourth can down next to the others. Glen tiptoed his way closer, curious to hear what his mother was saying to no one.

"Yup," her voice growing louder. "You left me and took all your promises with you. How many times did I tell you that I wanted to travel? All I wanted to do was go to Europe — Paris, London, Rome, anywhere." She raised her glass and gulped. In a mimicking voice she mocked, "Don't worry, Maretta. I'll take you someday. Someday, smhh, someday is dead." She slammed the glass down and it spit.

Glen snuck up behind his mother, mouthing silently to Tom, "thank you."

"I'll never get to Europe unless I go by myself. I'll have another," she told Tom.

Behind her, Glen shook his head no. He reached his

hands up and placed them gently on his mother's shoulders. "Mom?"

Marettas eyes opened wide. Her hands grasped the bar as she strained to turn her head around. "Glen, what are you doing here?"

"I came to get you, to take you home," he responded softly.

Maretta wobbled, Glen grabbed her. When she gained her composure, she stood up and looked behind her son. A lovely young woman, with silky blond hair, stood at the door watching them. Her warm essence radiated into Maretta and calmed her. "Who's that?"

Glen turned and the woman sprouted a warm smile, then waved shyly.

"That's Jenna," Glen said.

"Jenna?"

"My girlfriend," he added.

"You have a girlfriend," Maretta's said surprised.

"Yes."

"Why didn't you tell me?"

"There is a lot we need to catch up on," Glen said as he tried to maneuver Maretta away from the bar and towards the door.

Maretta dug her heels into the floor. "Whoa, I am not going home."

Glen drew in a deep breath. "Listen, Mom. I don't want you traveling alone."

"Why do you all think you know what is best for me?"

Glen rubbed the tips of his fingers into his forehead. "We

just worry, that's all. No one your age should be traveling alone."

"My age?" Maretta fired back, throwing her hands to her hips.

Glen looked at his mother and knew he needed to think fast, before she either made a bigger scene than she already had, or bolted for the car. The lunch crowd began to file in to the restaurant. Glen looked at Jenna who stood patiently waiting.

"Listen, what if I told you that I will take you to Europe?"

"Really?" Maretta let her hands fall to her sides. "You would do that?"

Glen smiled; relieved he found the key to her stubbornness. "Yes, anywhere you want to go. We'll go later this year."

Maretta thought about it, looked her son in the eye to see if he was being truthful. She felt love radiate out of the same dark-brown eyes Charlie had. She weighed her options, "Okay, just let me grab my purse."

Maretta turned and pulled her bag up from the floor. She paused and looked at the cans of beer still hanging out. "I'm going to Europe and Glen has a girlfriend. A girlfriend, can you believe that? You never know, Europe can be a romantic place to propose marriage," she winked at the cans.

Chapter 17

The familiar hum of the refrigerator was comforting. A delightful, warm breeze blew into the kitchen window. Outside, climbing hydrangea wrapped around the pillars of the teak pergola, buds just starting to burst open. Maretta hummed along with the birds chirping songs.

She lifted a dishtowel from the countertop, draped it over her nose and inhaled the sweet scent of home. The escapades of the past few days and the drama from last night, when they returned to the house, made her chuckle inside.

"Mom, the backdoor is open," Glen noticed as soon as they pulled Sofia into the driveway, Jenna following behind in the rental car.

"Well, I didn't leave it that way," Maretta defended herself. She was feeling particularly sensitive after she found out that her eldest son called in silver alert to find her. *A silver alert, can you imagine? I will never be able to drive through New Jersey again for fear they may arrest me and take me to a hospital thinking I am someone living with Alzheimer's. Tom the bartender made out well for calling me in.*

"Wait here," he insisted. He eased out of the car, flashed a 'wait' hand signal to Jenna, and went to the backdoor his back hunched over like a member of the swat team.

She was grateful she didn't actually call the real cops. The 'thief' turned out to be Andy.

"Well, when I heard Mom was going it alone, I started to worry. I flew in as fast as I could. I just got here an hour ago," Andy informed them.

Maretta's heart warmed just thinking about how comforting it was to see her two sons come out of the house. *They really do care*, she thought.

"Can I come in?" Joan asked, poking her head through the backdoor. "Is it safe?"

"Yes, you can come in," Maretta replied as if she were waved the dishtowel in the air like a white flag. "Want some coffee?"

Joan took a seat at the kitchen table while Maretta poured two steaming cups of java.

"The boys are still sleeping," Maretta whispered.

"Boys?" Joan asked.

"Yes, Andy flew in last night too," Maretta beamed.

"Paul said Glen brought a woman with him," Joan fished.

"Yes, isn't it exciting!" Maretta giggled like a schoolgirl.

"Knock, knock," Connie said as she let herself in.

"How did you know we were back?" Joan asked.

"Oh please, you know what a small town this is. Tom saw you driving in last night." She paused and looked at the new dos. "Love the hair! So, tell me, did you have fun?"

Joan and Maretta looked at each other, and then grinned like Cheshire cats.

"Thank goodness you're back," Ann said as she barged in. She stopped abruptly. "Oh my God. What happened to your hair?"

"Like it?" Maretta twirled in place. She didn't give Ann enough time to critique their color choices. "Would you two like some coffee?"

"Yes, please," said Connie.

"None for me," Ann replied and sat at the table. "I'm so relieved your back safely."

"Yes, Connie, we had fun," Joan started and proceeded to recap their travels. Maretta interjected to elaborate on their stories. Together they weaved a quilt of their experiences.

Ann and Connie laughed, gasped for breath and added, "Oh my."

"Poor George."

Joan explained that her son called the pancake restaurant and they promised to track down George and explain that she had to leave town due to an emergency.

"I want a pair," Connie commented.

Joan pulled out her yellow cheery glasses, "Aren't they great? So, tell us Connie, did you have a good time while we were gone?"

Connie blushed and looked away. "Well," she began, hesitating. "It started out fun but then it crashed and burned."

"Why, what happened?" Maretta asked.

"Well, Harold turned into an eighteen-year-old bronco once he started taking that supercharge pill. He couldn't get enough. They must put pheromones or something in those pills too. All of a sudden, ladies were approaching him, everywhere we went. You know what he told me? 'There are a lot of women that need to be satisfied,' and 'maybe I should share him.' So, I told him that I had my fill, go."

"Good for you."

"Well, I decided that I am going to take piano lessons," Ann said, wanting to share her news.

"Piano?" Joan repeated. "I've always wanted to play the guitar. We used to have volunteers come and play the guitar at the nursing home. It was so soothing."

"I used to play the flute, a long time ago," Connie said. "Did you play an instrument Maretta?"

"No, never really thought about it. I bet the drums would be fun," Maretta answered.

"Good Lord, what's next? Are we going to form a rock band?" Joan joked.

"Good morning," Glen said entering the room holding Jenna's hand. "Umm, this is my girlfriend, Jenna."

"Nice to meet you," Maretta's friends said as they looked Jenna over.

"Coffee?" Maretta asked.

"No, thanks, Mom. We're going to go to the diner for breakfast. I thought I would show Jenna around town. Do you mind if I take Sophia?"

"Go ahead, but watch out for the paparazzi," Maretta replied.

"They're relentless," Joan added.

Glen smiled and kissed his Mom on the cheek. She

handed him the keys. Jenna gave her a warm squeeze. "It was nice meeting all of you."

"Nice meeting you, too," they chimed, and then held their breath until the back door closed behind the two.

They huddled around the table like a football team.

"He has a girlfriend?" Connie snickered.

"Yes, I am over the moon," Maretta said. "And, it gets better. They are going to take me to Europe. Somewhere romantic." She slapped her hands together, swooning.

"Europe? What part?" Ann asked.

"Not sure," Maretta replied.

Silence fell between them.

Joan looked at Connie.

Connie looked at Ann.

Ann looked at Maretta. "I want to go."

"Me, too," added Connie.

"Me, three," said Joan.

"What about your husband?" Maretta questioned Ann.

"He can take care of himself. He doesn't listen to anything I say. He doesn't want to do anything except play golf, watch golf and nap." Ann sat back and let the jumbled thoughts in her head fall where they may. The vulnerability she felt lessened when she saw signs of compassion on the faces of her friends.

Andy shuffled into the kitchen, wiping the sleep from his eyes. "Good morning."

"Good morning," the four greeted him.

"Andy, we are going to form a rock band. Want to be our lead singer?" Joan joked.

"Umm," Andy stalled, reaching for a coffee cup. "I may have to get back to you on that."

"Yeah," Maretta said, "and I have the perfect name for our band, Cool Grannies!"

A Message from the Author

Thank you for reading this book, I hope you enjoyed it.
Would you like to see the Cool Grannies go on another trip?
Kindly leave a short review on
Amazon and/or Goodreads

You can continue to follow the Cool Grannies on their
Facebook page and their Twitter account: @CoolGrannies
and their website: www.coolgrannies.com

Do you know some Cool Grannies?
Share their story and use the hashtag #CoolGrannies
I look forward to hearing about the Cool Grannies you know.

To learn more about me, you can find me at
www.susanallisondean.com

Made in the USA
Columbia, SC
03 February 2019